# A Song of Love

Celia Latz

Tampa, Florida

**A Song of Love**

Published by Gatekeeper Press
7853 Gunn Hwy., Suite 209
Tampa, FL 33626
www.GatekeeperPress.com

Copyright © 2024 by Celia Latz
sonjahl@protonmail.com

Cover Art by Tamar Kander

Tamar Kander is a painter who has a studio just outside Bloomington, Indiana, where she lives with her husband and several animals. Galleries representing Tamar's work are located in Santa Fe NM, Winnetka IL and Indianapolis, IN. For a look at Tamar's' recent work and to view a list of the public collections in which she is included, please view: www.tamarkander.com



ISBN (paperback): 9781662955839
ISBN (hardback): 9781662955822
eISBN: 9781662955846

Library of Congress Control Number: 2024946725

# Contents

# A Song of Love

The island village of Lento clings to a rocky wall that descends to the Ionian Sea on the Eastern shore of Sicily. Its stone houses seem to grip the cliffs like its tenacious inhabitants holding on to their traditions. The village was a perfect picture on the surface when seagulls bobbed on the blue water like painted decoys, and life followed the predictable timing of the tolling of church bells. Yellow dogs lounged on the pavement outside the *macelleria* waiting for the butcher to toss out a bone to gnaw as lazy shadows moved slowly across the piazza until the sun eased under the horizon at the end of each languorous day.

That rhythm was broken with the onset of a worldwide pandemic, and with it came a wave of change. Seagulls that once congregated at the port, began strutting through the village like thugs. They pecked pigeons, eating them alive while the victims suffered with glazed eyes and people watched in disgust, sidestepping the remains that littered the streets like oily rags. Restaurants closed due to the pandemic, diminishing the glut of table scraps the gulls had grown to rely upon. Yet there was still plenty of garbage to strew over the pavers of the narrow streets. The gulls ripped open garbage bags with insatiable appetites and became louder and bolder as time passed. Villagers were awakened during the night by their uncanny noise that sounded like whelping dogs and bawling cats.

Sometimes these hearty, white-breasted birds seemed to cackle and laugh mockingly, as if only they knew what catastrophes would follow, welcoming chaos, and relishing their exclusive knowledge of impending doom. The gulls' belligerence resonated throughout the village, and people seemed affected by the same mysterious entity that brought about the disaccord. The villagers' once complacent lives became focused on malicious gossip, conspiracy theories, and hateful resentment during the quarantine that lasted over two long years.

Maria owns a *trattoria* on a back street in Lento. Trattoria Da Maria is a popular meeting place known not only for its customary homestyle cooking but also for its owner, a glum, obese woman in her early thirties. Little is known about her private life, leaving ample space to fill with fictitious ingenuity. Her classic Grecian features are debased by a flat expression void of emotions, defying any suggestion of beauty. Clad in plain black dresses, without family or friends, she ignores her neighbors and lives alone in a house referred to by the villagers as "the hovel." She never found a need to install a telephone, let alone use an iPhone. Despite her apparent poverty, she mysteriously bought and remodeled the trattoria  and established a successful business on her own, providing fodder for gossip and speculation about where the money came from. The villagers delight in sharing theories, based on nothing, regarding the source of her funds, insinuating a secret sex life with a boss of the *Camorra*. Anyone who attempted to provoke and taunt her found no satisfaction in her lack of response. The fact that she is an excellent cook and efficient manager is too boring to talk about. Gossip is even spicier than the tasty food they consume in the trattoria that's in high demand. With no rent to pay and no one to take care of, she survived the loss of income during the painful period of social isolation. Now that life is returning to normal, Trattoria Da Maria is again open for business.

Sandra lives in Catania, the second-largest city in Sicily, an hour and a half north of Lento. She was sixteen when the news of a contagious disease was first reported, and she, like many others, thought it was just another Asian flu that would come and go. No one knew they would be confined to their homes, subjected to police control, allowed to go out only to the pharmacy or grocery, for an indeterminable length of time. The lack of social life was especially traumatic for teenagers who could no longer convene every evening in the piazza for aperitifs and verbal cacophony, but Sandra was immune to the effects of the quarantine. She created her own world in the realm of music, satisfied by the company of her passionate companion—a piano. Her social interaction was with her herbs and flowers and the mature, self-sufficient wisteria vine on the arbor next to her house. Her sole human contacts during the pandemic were with Maria, with whom she corresponded by mail, and her composition tutor from the conservatory, who had come to her home weekly before the pandemic and continued lessons on zoom for over a year during the quarantine. The in-person lessons had just recently resumed.

The quarantine ended at last, and Sandra was nineteen, free to travel to visit Maria in Lento. Unlike before, nothing could impede her from going: no more arguing with her parents for permission. They died of the virus, leaving a bittersweet memory, and Sandra savors her newly found independence. She planned the visit in delicious silence. During the past year of living alone, she adapted to silence that became an empty yearning to sate with music. Her time alone with the piano was a refuge from the disharmony of a chaotic world out of tune with her need for beauty and order. Each time she sat down to play, she left the turmoil of mundane drudgery behind, creating eloquent musical expression that transported her to an idyllic haven. But now physical transportation was again possible and she could visit Maria—not just to see her, but to tell her some important recent news—news she feared would upset Maria.

She reserved an Uber to go to the train station and bought a digital ticket for Lento online without speaking a word, but as she locked up the house, rode to the station, and rode the train, her internal conversation was lively. The train groaned out of Catania heading south as she gazed at the sea on the left side of the tracks. The entire coastline of the city is cut off by train tracks and a fence. Only one public beach is accessible by a dank entrance through an underpass next to the train station. What terrible planning, she thought. One could only view the sea through a chain-link fence, let alone stroll along the shore or wade in the water. The thought of this waste of a beautiful natural resource angered her as she simmered over whoever the urban planner was, and the administration that agreed to his plan. "He cut off the best asset of the city by inflicting his myopic stupidity on generations of Catanians and visitors to come!" She didn't moderate her emotional opinions, especially about nature and its destruction.

Some tourists with suitcases got off the train at the first stop, Fontanarossa, the airport, before the tracks veered away from the coast, entering rural countryside. She watched the scenery flow by thinking how it hadn't changed much since she took the same trip three years ago to see Maria. The orange orchards were vibrant and cultivated, in contrast to the barren swath of land along the tracks where prickly pear cacti had been hacked down. Sandra observed them lying flat on the ground, limp, and drained of color like dying soldiers on a battlefield. She focused on the orchards composed of the glossy green trees in straight rows, with vivid orange fruit populating the branches. Plants flourished in the rich volcanic soil around the active volcano Etna that loomed in the distance like a handsome criminal. The fecund earth was cultivated by farmers who respected their land in contrast to the public land that was sullied and downtrodden like an innocent, abused girl.

The train didn't stop at the next station. As it rolled slowly by the platform, Sandra noticed gnarled electrical wiring and jagged plastic pipes protruding from the broken cement walls, serving no recognizable purpose.

Half-finished empty buildings without glass where windows should be stood like zombies in weedy fields. These were newly built structures, abandoned before being used, erected to give the appearance of industrious activity when in fact, there was no intention to finish them. Funds allotted by the national government to stimulate Sicilian economy ended up in the pockets of local "politicians" and the Camorra that flourished on the profits from the seeds of corruption sown and harvested year after year. Those with some power who attempted to uproot the dishonesty, like the magistrate Giovani Falcone, ended up dead and buried in the same earth they fought to protect.

The dismal scenery stoked her anxiety. She had big news to tell Maria, but remembered how Maria had admonished her regarding men the last time she saw her. "Take time. Never let a boy lead you down the wrong path! They can seem good, and then turn bad." The memory of Maria's warning resonated in her mind and body as the train arrived at Priolo Melilla, the last station before her destination. This place made the last stop seem like Eden in comparison. Here there was nothing but petroleum cisterns in a jungle of pipes and cement extending for miles without a spot of green or evidence of life.

She prepared herself to get off at the next station, the stop closest to Lento. The anxiety over the devastation of nature piqued and she didn't want to appear agitated when she met Maria. Closing her eyes, she thought of a serene melodious theme of an opus she had been composing and breathed deeply. Soon there would be other problems to confront that she had some control over.

Lento is about a half-kilometer walk from the station, with a bridge that unites the island to the mainland. She had written to Maria to let her know of her arrival but wondered if she got the letter and if she would be there to meet her. The train's brakes screeched as it entered the station while Sandra arose from her seat and made her way toward the closest door to exit. When the train jerked to a stop, she stepped off with an overnight bag and a package of cannoli. As she walked toward the exit of the station, she felt sure Maria would be there, and in fact, there she was. Her short, albeit imposing figure dressed in black dominated the scene. Sandra was surprised to see how Maria had gone from stout to obese since the last time she saw her and tried to hide her dismay, but Maria knew what Sandra thought by the way she pretended not to notice the obvious.

"Don't worry about me, Sandra. Food is my best friend. All that's important to me is that you are happy and healthy. Look at you—so skinny and pretty. Who would think I'm your mother?"

"I brought you some cannoli from Prestipino, your favorite *pasticceria*." Maria reached for the package with porcine eyes.

"Grazie! No one makes cannoli like Prestipino! Now, *andiamo*—let's go to my trattoria—it's time for lunch. I hope you're hungry."

Maria's trattoria was beginning to return to normal after the lengthy closure, once again filled with hungry customers starving for social interaction. Sandra followed Maria down the narrow street to her mother's trattoria and to the same table where they sat three years ago when Sandra came the first time with questions. Maria, in her open simplicity, had answered Sandra's questions with painful honesty that bonded the two. It was this quality—Maria's sincerity—that especially endeared her to Sandra. This time, it was Sandra's turn to open up but she wasn't emotionally prepared. Instead, she talked about the loss of Paolo and Elena Montesi, her adoptive parents who had died a year ago.

"How have you gotten along? I'm sorry for Elena and Paolo—the Montesis—good people," Maria said with reverence.

"They were. They didn't have to die, but they wouldn't get the vaccine. They thought it was an exaggeration, invented to manipulate people, and to enrich pharmaceutical companies. I begged them to get it, but they said I was brainwashed to believe it was safe. They didn't even wear masks and kept quietly inviting their friends over who risked going out for their famous cocktail parties. How ironic that I'm here, and they are gone."

"Not ironic! Logical. They listened to gossip! Why would they think the same doctors who they've known for years would suddenly want to shoot them with something to hurt them?"

"It doesn't make sense. They were good people, but they didn't think about spreading the virus to others by disregarding the rules."

"You were only eighteen when they died. How did you make it all alone in that big house without any help? I worried about you every day."

"I wasn't really alone—I had your letters, my piano, my lessons, and my plants to take care of."

"Now I can take care of you!" Maria turned her attention to the door of the kitchen. "Here comes our lunch. I had some caponata made for you, with grilled tuna." The waiter sauntered toward them and placed two plates on the table with precise movements, then stood by for confirmation that the food met their standards. Sandra tasted a few bites anticipating the wholesome flavors the trattoria was known for. "Delicious! The sweet and sour undertones with the briny capers complement the tuna. Did you know some of the great composers were also great chefs, Maria? Rossini, for one . . . It takes artistic skill and an innate talent for composition to cook so well. You're an artist."

Maria fidgeted with her napkin, searching for words to change the subject. She couldn't imagine herself with artistic talent, and didn't know how to respond to praise or accept a compliment gracefully. When the plates were taken away, neither knew what to say. "Want some dessert?" Maria asked, breaking the silence.

"No, thank you. I'm looking forward to seeing where you live. You told me it's not fancy, but that's not important to me at all. I know you've lived there all your life, and I'm curious to see the room you slept in when you were little, and I want to learn more about your life."

"My house—not like what you're used to, but I hope you'll feel at home. It was my mother's house. She didn't die of the pandemic. Cancer killed her when I was twenty. My father died long before she did, when I was a kid—an accident at work. He was a construction worker. Let's go. It's not too far from here. "

As they walked, Maria vented. "People are going crazy. One of my waiters was robbed at knifepoint on payday after work, poor guy. The customers don't have manners like before—they order the waiters around like they're slaves—so rude. A neighbor's car was broken into just to steal a pack of cigarettes. These things didn't happen when I was a girl. People were nicer. But something that hasn't changed—the corruption. When I opened the trattoria, I didn't sign up for the vigilante protection . . . Then one night, someone broke in and tore it up. When I found the damage, there was already a guy there in a uniform waiting for me. He was one of those guards that puts little flyers in the doors of shops advertising their service. I always threw those paper scraps away. He said if I had paid for protection, this wouldn't have happened. So, I started paying a hundred euros every month even though I discovered from other shop owners that it was the same vigilante that vandalized my place, to make me sign up. That is how things work here. No one has the courage to denounce them."

"Can't you go to the police?" Sandra asked.

"Oh, Sandra, I'm sorry to tell you, the police do nothing. Everyone, including the police, are too afraid to raise their head. I either pay, or I'll find my place trashed again, or worse! It's useless–I have no power to fight it. Those guys are really bad."

Sandra listened in dismay to Maria's litany. At least it gave her more time to think about how to tell her news, which she planned to do the next day.

Maria's house was a longer walk from the trattoria than Sandra expected. Her accounts of vandalism and robbery gave the narrow streets an intimidating aspect that she didn't sense before. They meandered along the curving streets that disoriented Sandra. She lost all sense of direction and would not know her way back to the trattoria, or even to the main square. They entered a little courtyard where Maria noticed Sandra admiring the array of plants in terra-cotta pots of varied shapes and sizes—from hearty palms, lemon trees, and geraniums, to delicate little blue flowers, called *Occhi di Madonna*, and a variety of herbs that she used for cooking at the trattoria. There were also pots of different varieties of cacti that grow naturally in the area.

"Here we are. *Casa mia*!" Maria announced.

"Are these your plants?"

"My babies," Maria boasted.

"I love to take care of my plants too." Sandra stepped carefully around the plants, touching the leaves affectionately, smelling their scents as Maria jostled with a ring of keys to open the front door. The ground floor of the house was composed of a sitting room, Maria's bedroom, and a windowless bathroom that was needlessly large. The kitchen and another room were up a narrow stairway on the first floor. Maria had prepared the room upstairs with scrutiny, where Sandra would sleep for the first time in her mother's house. She knew well the luxury and elegance of the Montesi home and fretted over what Sandra might think of her humble abode, built into the rocky side of a hill.

"Thank you for inviting me to stay with you, Maria. Will I be in the room that was yours when you were growing up?"

"Yes. The one upstairs. I use my mother's old room now. Let's go to the living room and have some of those cannoli you brought. You need some dessert."

They sat on the same tattered furniture that had been in the house since Maria was born. She put the cardboard tray of cannoli on the coffee table, removed the cellophane wrapper, and edged the tray toward Sandra. "You first."

"I pity anyone who has never had a genuine cannolo," Sandra said before biting into the crisp shell. "The ricotta filling is barely sweetened, exalting the flavor of the fresh ricotta cheese. It's so good, I don't want to swallow it! The chewy candied pieces of orange rind add a touch of bitterness to the delicacy of the ricotta without overpowering the natural taste of the goat milk, and the bittersweet chocolate chips complete the symphony."

"Oh, Sandra. You say what I think, but I can't talk like you. You grew up well with the Montesi. That's the good thing."

"Mamma, I have missed you all my life. I feel like I'm finally home."

Maria tried to hide the emotion she felt when she heard Sandra call her "Mamma" but after a moment, she let words flow forth that she couldn't suppress.

"I missed all those years watching you grow up, combing your hair, cooking for you, walking you to school. I have cried almost all my tears, missing you so much, wishing we were together."

Sandra put her cannolo back on the tray and got up to sit next to Maria. She put her arms around her mother and embraced her. They both sensed a surge of love as tears dampened Maria's full cheeks.

"See? You still have some tears! It's good to have tears when we need to cry," Sandra murmured.

Maria responded with a brusque tone to disguise her vulnerability. "You must be tired from your trip today. You go hop into bed. Tomorrow will come soon."

Elegance and décor were far from Sandra's thoughts as she climbed the steep wooden steps to the upper floor. She admired the rustic furnishings of the bedroom and felt inherently at home with Maria, even though they had only met a few times. She opened the shutters, pulled back the white crocheted bedspread, nestled into the homespun sheets, and fell asleep. She was soon awakened by the screeching in the courtyard below her window.

"*Oh, Dio,*" she thought. "What is going on with those birds?" Normally, inappropriate noise could be dealt with. Maria could ask her neighbors to turn down the volume of their TVs, or call the police after 10:00 p.m. for loud music from the bar on the corner. At least these problems could be solved by rules that were respected. They were annoying problems, but solvable within the realm of lawful reality. But she was helpless to stop the inane din of the gulls. She could only wonder what shift in nature had provoked them, as if they were instruments of a sinister entity.

She lie awake with the window open, watching the full moon, feeling its soothing presence like a reliable companion. Not a sigh of breeze entered. The moon's pale elegance illuminated the room, consoling her for the lack of air. She could clearly see the outline of the picture on the vanity, taken at her first piano recital when she was nine years old. The light reflected on the silver frame reminded her of how Maria's eyes glowed when she gave her the photo three years ago. It was a rare glimpse of tenderness that Maria rarely displayed.

Sandra got out of bed to get a glass of milk, which usually helped her fall asleep. When she opened the refrigerator door, the artificial light from the appliance reflected on the kitchen's stone wall, which was merely the exposed side of the mountain. She marveled at this primitive, natural feature of the old house and touched the rough stones with the tips of her fingers. It was cooler in this room, so she sat down at the table to drink the milk. In a Biology course at school, she had learned that maternal milk has tryptophan that produces serotonin that induces sleep in babies and adults. She had never been nursed but thought maybe this cold, bovine milk would help her fall asleep. She finished the glass, rinsed it out, went back to bed, and stretched her long legs on the coarse flaxen sheets. By now, the gulls had moved on to heckle someone else.

Sandra relaxed in the quietude, playing "Liebestraum" in her mind. Her fingers moved as she touched the smooth ivory keys on an imaginary piano, thinking of her fiancé's arms around her, and his dark eyes, so deep and expressive that when he looked into her eyes, she felt his soul within her. Slowly, the pensive notes of "The Dream of Love" lured her to sleep.

Maria was not awakened by the gulls. Her cumbersome body sunk into the mattress as she slept soundly in her room on the ground floor, with the shutters closed and barred. Instead of making her feel confined, the barrier provided a sense of protection. She was thirty-two years old and had never desired a man or considered sex could be anything but something painful, to fear. She had given birth to Sandra when she was thirteen years old, and to her, the past nineteen years seemed like a grueling lifetime. Her childhood ended the day a boy called Checco used her as the object of his unofficial coming-of-age ceremony. He was a timid boy who Maria liked because of his shyness, until that day.

He was introverted and appeared to be intellectual—an aloof loner—making him a target for the other boys in the class. When they passed him in the hall, they flicked their ear lobes with their forefingers, which was code to call out a homosexual. "Checco, Checca," they jeered. His nickname was close to Checca—a derisive slangy term meaning homosexual. They dared him to seduce a girl—any girl. "Prove you can do it," they snarled. Maria was in the same class as the boy, where he had noticed her bright eyes and shy smile, and he decided she would be his accomplice.

When he invited her to walk along the shore with him, she sweetly consented. He took her hand and led her toward the sea, to the only beach of Lento, the Cala Rossa. The touch of his delicate hand, a tress of dark hair fallen out of place over an eye, his slender body, and confident strides, excited her. She looked at the blue sea below and was eager to stand on the stony shore with this boy, and perhaps feel his tender lips on hers. She felt a luscious warmth in her belly that made her ache to be touched.

He clenched her hand and led her down the steps to the beach, then pulled her along the wall with urgency, until they reached a scruffy inlet, apart from the romantic shoreline. She was surprised by this detour, but thoughts of danger were remote. He was the one boy in her class she had a crush on because of his kindness and sensitivity. But then he stopped and looked at her oddly. He no longer seemed like the same boy, and her sweet smile transformed into a blank stare. With robotic movements, he forced her to the ground and held her down. She struggled to push him off but he held her firmly under his weight.

"Stop!" she cried, but her timid plea grew to screams in a fit of panic. Her calls for help were muted as he tried to muffle them without seeing the fright in her eyes or understanding her resistance. When he finished, he felt relieved it was over—he had accomplished his end of a deal and could report back to the bullies and put an end to their jeering. But why did Maria put up a fight, and why was she whimpering? he wondered. Her reaction surprised him. He thought she liked him and that it would be easy . . . maybe even pleasant. This was not how he thought sex would be.

"Don't tell anyone," he ordered. His effort to appear in control seemed glib to Maria. "Everyone does this. It's natural; this is our secret." Maria couldn't respond. She was sobbing from shock, shame, and a sharp pain in her bleeding vagina. She felt permeated with his smell . . . the stench of his sweat mixed with the odor of discarded garbage. She had been raped in a squalid place—a cove for rats. This smell of shame and pain became a lasting memory that stained her existence. In the following weeks, no matter how much she washed and scrubbed, she felt dirty and humiliated. Anger grew within her, reminding her constantly of the painful struggle. She mocked herself—ashamed of the romantic desire to be kissed and the sweet expectation that she had experienced for the first and last time, lost forever.

"I'm so stupid. I trusted him and he's so bad. What is wrong with me?"

After two months, she noticed a change in her body. Her periods had just begun, and now they had already stopped. She had kept the secret as the boy had demanded, hoping the memory would disappear if ignored. Now she had to face another terrifying reality and tell her mother what happened. The reaction to Maria's "confession" was almost as painful as the rape. Her mother was not so concerned about her daughter's plight, as to how to deal with this inconvenient problem. She knew that an illegal abortion wasn't an option—but even worse, Maria's pregnancy would bring shame on them both. Maria would never be considered "a good girl." At least her father was no longer alive to suffer this indignity. The truth had to be hidden. Again, Maria was told, this time by her mother, "Don't tell anyone."

Maria was withdrawn from school and existed in her mothers' house like a fugitive: powerless, a container for an alien growing within her. Her growing anger devoured her day after day. For a few weeks, she waited like a caged animal.

"Mama, I'm scared. I don't want to have a baby! Why can't I get an abortion?"

"Because you could go to jail, or even die. Remember Antonia? She didn't die of a disease. That was a lie. She was pregnant and the woman here who fixes these things messed up. Antonia got a fever, and stopped going to school. Her teacher didn't believe her mother's excuse and reported the absence to the police. The police began to ask around about Antonia and heard gossip about the midwife. This led to inquiries, hoping to discover a crime, but the midwife would not speak.

They went to Antonia's house in their Carabinieri uniforms and interrogated her while she sweat with fever in her bed. She didn't answer their questions and before leaving, they warned, 'If there's a drop of oil in the water, it will rise to the top.' So she stayed home, afraid to go to the doctor, and bled to death. The same could happen to you. Who was this boy, Maria?"

"Everyone calls him Checco. I don't know his real name. He's in my class. Does he know I'm pregnant?"

"How would he know? He better not know. Everyone would talk and you'd never get married. I see the boys sitting at the café after school, laughing. He's probably one of them and hasn't even noticed you've been absent. You should know better. I didn't bring you up to get into this kind of trouble."

Maria burned with resentment. "I thought he was nice! I'd be in school now if it wasn't for him! He's ruined my life! I just want this thing gone!"

"Maria. You have made a mistake and now you are having a baby."

The words "you're having a baby" hit Maria like a stone.

"We'll take care of this, Maria. Don't talk to anyone—we'll take care of this somehow."

Maria's mother went to the priest in their parish for support and bluntly explained her daughter's predicament to Padre Ernesto. "What can we do with the baby? Maria's like a baby herself. I cannot bring up another kid with no help." The priest listened with stoic patience. He was expressionless, ready to utter the usual platitudes, until an idea brought life to his face. He spoke of a childless couple—the Signori Montesi who lived in Catania.

"I know them well," he said. "Paolo Montesi is my brother, and I think they would be interested in adopting this baby. They are not so young anymore, but his wife, Elena, has always regretted not being able to have children."

Soon after the meeting with the priest, Elena Montesi contacted Maria's mother and offered to take Maria into their home until the birth and with the girl's consent, adopt the baby. Maria was informed she'd be staying with the Montesi on the same day a car came to take her away. She felt she had already lived her life and died, thrown away, abandoned by her own mother without a hug or loving words, confirming her sense of dirtiness and guilt. Not even her mother could embrace her now.

Nineteen years later, Maria sleeps in her dark room, behind bars, trapped within a joyless body, while the beautiful product of her pain sleeps in the room above, dreaming of love.

# La Casa Montesi

The introduction of Maria to the Montesi had taken place as a business transaction. She was a package, wrapped up in shame, stamped with doom, and delivered into the hands of strangers. It was a cordial transaction. Intense emotions were concealed behind nervous smiles and perfunctory handshaking. Maria's mother introduced the couple to her. "This is Signora Elena Montesi and her husband, Dr. Paolo Montesi. You will be living with them until you have the baby. They have everything you need. Be grateful you can leave with them today. This is a good solution. Goodbye, Maria." She was directed into the back seat of the car and looked through the window at her mother who watched her sitting in the gleaming Fiat sedan as it drove away. She appeared detached at the sight of her daughter leaving home, then walked on stiffened legs into her house, threw herself onto Maria's bed, and sobbed.

The drive north to Catania was a series of curves and hills. Maria had been feeling dizzy from the pregnancy, but this ride caused waves of nausea.

"Stop! I'm sick."

Dr. Montesi slowed down and pulled the car off to the side of the road. Maria opened the car door just in time before vomiting on the dusty shoulder of the road. Signora Montesi got out and ceremoniously patted Maria's back. She took a tissue from her leather designer purse, ready to wipe Maria's tears and clean her lips. Her attempt to hug the girl was awkward, and Maria abruptly got back into the car to avoid physical contact with the awkward stranger. She was numb and preferred it that way. She would not feel vulnerable again. She was not a girl anymore. She was not a woman. She was no one now, nothing but an organism to host something growing inside her body, something she hated. Above all, she hated Checco, who seemed to her like a cruel alien from a sinister place in the universe sent to destroy her.

"Maria, we're almost here, dear. Look—that's our house up there." Signora Montesi pointed to a house high on the hill overlooking the sea and a rocky beach. Then she turned her vapid gaze toward the seashore. "See those big boulders in the water?" She spoke as if reading from a brochure addressing a group of tourists. "Those were thrown at Odysseus by the Cyclops, as the story goes, but the Cyclops had been blinded by Odysseus, who managed to dodge every rock."

Catania was much bigger than the little village where Maria had lived. There were cafés, people sitting at tables outside, and shops along the main road, Via Etnea. She knew there was a university here—the one she probably would've gone to before her life was upended. The Fiat drove up Via dei Ciclopi, turned into the driveway, and parked under an arbor dripping with lavender wisteria blossoms from a thick trunk. Signora Montesi helped Maria out of the back seat and accompanied her to the front door while her husband got her suitcase out of the trunk. Maria took in the size of the house. She saw a terrace and balconies facing the sea and hoped her room would be one with a balcony. When the solid front door was pushed open, she stepped into a new world.

She saw what a contrast this house was to her mother's home. The elegant, modern furniture in neutral tones was arranged for conversations in the spacious living room. Original paintings hung harmoniously on the walls in contrast to the single, stained print of the Virgin Mary in her mother's dim living room. Large windows framed the views outside, flooding the rooms with light. Shelves were not cluttered with knickknacks, but filled with books. A sleek black grand piano occupied a corner of the room.

Her mother's house, with its small windows and thick stone walls, was dark. Cumbersome furniture faced the TV, which was the main focus of the room. The shutters were usually closed during the day to shield the upholstery from the rays of sun, leaving a crack just big enough to allow a little light to slip in. The tattered fabric was hardly worth protecting, but the shutters were kept closed out of habit.

"Come upstairs. We'll show you your room," Signora Montesi lilted. She led Maria up the stairs, who felt the novelty of her silent footsteps upon the plush carpeting. Signora Montesi stopped in front of a bedroom at the end of the hall and Maria walked into the room, straight to the balcony. For the first time in weeks, she took a breath of air, appreciating this most basic function of survival. For a moment, the briny air and the view of the sea made her forget her fate. Gulls gracefully skimmed over the surface of the calm, blue water below.

Dr. Montesi placed Maria's beat-up suitcase on the bench at the foot of the bed. A yellow comforter with colorful cushions gave a warm aura to the room, but Maria felt wary of the tasteful décor. She had never been in such a place and the sight of her pathetic suitcase embarrassed her. There was even a bathroom all to herself, with bright yellow and blue tiles. Never had she imagined a bathroom could be bright and beautiful and for her exclusive use.

"We'll leave you alone for a while to rest and freshen up. Come down around seven for dinner. Va bene?" Elena's forced glee, as if all this was normal, made Maria feel even more alone and out of place. She closed the door and moved a chair to sit facing the balcony. This was the first time she was so far from her own village. She was a stranger in this new home, and new town, and with new people—rich people—to live with, just as she was a stranger to her own body. A tiny bundle of cells had taken control of it. She had control of nothing.

"At seven I will go down for dinner with these people. Why am I here? Will every day be like this until I expel the thing in me? And then, after that? Will I go home, back to school? Ha! Nothing will be the same again. Checco ruined my life, and he goes on like before, like I never existed."

The thought of him made her feel unclean and disgusted with herself. She sat immobile with her anger, barely breathing, until she shivered from a chilling breeze as a cloud covered the sun. She had never felt so alone. The thing inside her weighed like a boulder, crushing her hopes, killing her dreams. As she looked down at the shoreline, all she could see in her mind's eye was the filthy, rocky patch littered with garbage where her childhood ended.

She stood up to go downstairs—down to another layer of hell—and sat down dutifully at the dining table on the chair Dr. Montesi pulled out for her. The table was set with silverware and porcelain dishes placed on a white tablecloth. An arrangement of fresh flowers and glowing candles sat in the center of the table. This was unreal. Maria had seen such elegant tables only on TV.

"Maria, you look a little pale. Do you feel okay?"

"No. I'm not hungry."

"But, you must eat. Think of the baby."

"Think of the *baby*? That's all anyone thinks of!"

"No, Maria, we want you to be happy here. Please have some dinner. We have a lot to talk about—we're very happy you're here."

"Why are you glad I'm here?"

"The priest in Lento, Padre Ernesto, is my husband's brother. He reached out to us about your situation after your mother went to him for help. We understand it would've been inconvenient for you to carry the pregnancy through in the village. Your mother wanted to protect you by removing you from that place—you know—where everyone talks about everyone else. You've done nothing wrong. We're sorry this terrible thing has happened to you and we want to help. My husband, Paolo, is a lawyer, so he can take care of any eventual problems for you or your mother."

"But, I don't understand why you're doing this. You don't even know us."

"Paolo and I have never been blessed with children. Having you here with us is a joy. We hope you'll feel at home, and we will be here for you until the baby is born."

"And then, what?"

"And then, the baby will need a home. Your mother can't take care of the child and you are so young. We hope you will consider this home as your baby's home. We want to adopt this child."

Maria didn't respond. She was digesting these words like rocks in her stomach. Now, she began to understand the reason for their attention. Now, this all made sense. Yes. She was just a container for something more important than herself. This would be her only reason to live—to grow the thing, and give it away. She couldn't think of the uninvited blob inside her as a child.

"The precious thing," she thought to herself. She felt foolish for thinking they might care about her. "The knot of throbbing cells is all they care about."

"Of course, you can think about this. We just want you to know that you have this option, and that we'd be good parents for your baby."

"Your baby." These words resonated in Maria's mind.

"You want this baby in exchange for my staying here? You can have it! I don't want it, and it's not my baby! It's nothing but a horrible mistake!"

An awkward silence dangled over the table until Paolo spoke.

"This is not a business transaction. But, you have something we want, and we can help you have what you want. It can be good for us, and good for you. You're free to—"

Signora Montesi interrupted. "It seems you've already decided, Maria. We need to make our agreement official—it'll be less stressful for all of us to have a plan. The sooner, the better."

Maria understood the urgency of their offer. She wanted to get the ordeal over with too. Suddenly, she felt the thing in her had some value after all—at least to someone. They wanted the one thing that had ruined her life, and she could hide in the comfort of their home until she would be rid of it.

"Va bene. How do we do this?" Maria asked.

"We have papers to sign. It's not complicated," assured Dr. Montesi. "You will have nothing to worry about."

Elena Montesi arose from the table and returned with a dessert on a platter that resembled a black cannon ball.

"This is a specialty here—it's called a "bomba.""

Maria cut through the hardened chocolate surface, into the cool, soft filling and savored the bittersweet flavors. Just as she had breathed in the fresh sea air earlier that day, she felt a pleasant sensation.

Maria felt confined in the Montesi home, but not like she had felt in her mother's home in Lento. She was now aware that within her body, she possessed an object of desire. She owned something of value, and therefore deserved the commodities and attention she now commanded. This new status showed in the way she sat passively like a stump on the sofa in the elegant living room, how she hunkered over the dinner plate, avoiding eye contact or conversation. Her goal was to consume, pay up, and be set free in just seven more months. She had no interest in the paintings on the walls, and never read even the titles of the books on the shelves. She left the room when Elena sat down to play the piano and could not understand how anyone would want such a big noisy piece of furniture in their house. She sat at the balcony of her room each morning and watched the gulls flying over the cove in their individual flight patterns, not like starlings that fly together in harmony. The gulls flew randomly, scattered across the sky. She noticed they had become noisier. Their rude squawking, complaining, and taunting was as random as their flight.

"Maria . . ." called Mrs. Montesi. "Why don't you come downstairs?"

"No!" Maria grunted with a tone as harsh as the gulls.

# Sandra

Almost seven months after Maria's arrival in the Montesi house, she was forty pounds heavier. This weight on her short frame transformed her from a petite, spirited girl into a sulking heap. She was void of interest in anything. In fact, she scorned the endeavors of the Montesi to expose her to art and music and literature. To their disapproval, she passed her time on the sofa watching soap operas and eating the specialty sweets and at least four cannoli a day from the town's best pasticceria, Prestipino.

Signora Esposito  habitually played the piano after dinner and hoped Maria would show interest. "Maria, I'd be happy to give you lessons if you'd like to play."

"No!" Maria responded. After cleaning her plate and devouring dessert, Maria went to her room to sit at the balcony, staring at the sky with dull eyes while the music drifted up into her room. She endured it with resentment for months, until one evening she pulled herself up off her chair, trod toward the stairs and descended heavily, into the living room. "Stop!" she demanded. Elena's hands suspended over the keyboard as she looked at Maria with shock.

"What's wrong?"

"I think it's happening! All this water just came out and . . ."

"Paolo! It's time! Get the car!" Elena rushed to phone the hospital, then grabbed the bag of layette items that had been prepared in advance. Maria groaned from the intense ache in her lower back. She had never seen Elena so emotional, yet fiercely efficient. Elena was more excited than Maria, but she tried to calm the girl, knowing it was a futile effort to stifle the moaning. Though she had never experienced childbirth, she understood instinctively that these beastly sounds were natural in childbearing. Yet she felt uncomfortable and embarrassed by the animalistic tones that gradually increased in volume at regular intervals. Paolo was agitated as well, but kept his focus on driving to the Cannizzaro hospital. With each wave of contraction, Maria bellowed louder, like an enraged elephant.

The labor lasted longer than usual, and given Maria's young age and weight, she was carefully monitored throughout the long and tortuous ordeal. The Cannizzaro hospital was oriented toward aid and respect to girls who had been raped. It was not only close to the Montesi home, but chosen by Elena for its ethics. Elena stayed by Maria'a side, smoothing back her hair damp with sweat from her face, until finally, the top of the slick head of the baby appeared. With one last trumpeting wail, Maria pushed the baby from her body and fell back on the pillow, feeling that her uterus had been expelled with the baby. She abandoned herself to the next phase of her uncertain future, lying on the crumpled bed, bleeding profusely, and gazing at the ceiling.

Elena removed her hand from Maria's head and fixed her eyes on the tiny writhing body. "My daughter," she heard herself say. "My baby, Sandra." Paolo put his arm around Elena. "So you've named her Sandra. Nice."

All the attention that had previously been aimed at Maria was abruptly transferred to the newborn baby: a turning point for everyone. The newborn already had a name chosen by Elena, excluding Maria from the choice. Sandra was now the treasure that the Montesi held. She belonged to them. Maria no longer contained what they wanted, and soon, she would return to her village, empty and alone, to her mother who no longer considered her a sweet child, but an inconvenient burden. Added to this, the doctor told her she would never be able to have children again. Maria watched Elena touch the baby's tiny fingers and call her by name. She felt an unexpected sense of loss and sadness. Reality rocked her—this baby was her first and would be her last. She would never experience motherhood or ever fall in love. She was sure of that.

"Elena," Maria whispered. "Promise me you will tell my baby who I am someday, when she's old enough to understand. I want her to know. Promise me."

"But there is no reason the child should ever know. You agreed. I . . . we are the parents now. You signed the papers . . ."

"I will find her and tell her myself if you don't. It is the right thing. It's the truth."

Elena looked at Paolo. "Elena, someday our age difference will become obvious to everyone. We can't hide the fact that she is adopted."

Realizing what she must do, Elena mumbled, "I promise."

# The Confession

The milk had produced the desired effect. Sandra slept through the rest of the night and awakened in the morning, refreshed, but still apprehensive about telling Maria about the news—the reason for her visit. She hoped to see the rare glow in her eyes. Today, maybe her news would lighten the mood, but she was afraid it would have the opposite effect, because of Maria's aversion to anything romantic. Maria had never been interested in marriage or men and Sandra understood that the humiliation of being raped, the hatred of Checco, and the painful birth still haunted her.

Sandra heard the blunt sounds of Maria thumping around downstairs, starting the day in her graceless manner. Her elegance was in striking contrast to Maria but the two women had a tacit connection. She crept down the steps to greet her mother.

"Good morning, Mamma." She never called Elena "Mamma" but relished saying the word now. The Montesi had told Sandra she was adopted when she was six years old, but Sandra was too surprised to process the reality. The shocking revelation upset Sandra to the point that she didn't want to ever meet her natural mother, and wondered why she was given away at birth, resenting the person who had rejected her. As she lived with this fact over the years, she thought of Elena and Paolo as her carekeepers and thrived in their affluent world. When Sandra and Maria first met, both mother and daughter wondered how they could be even distantly related. Maria was short and heavy with a blunt character and little education. Sandra was tall and graceful with the bright eyes that Maria lost long ago.

"Mornin,' Sandra. How'd you sleep?"

"Very well, until those obnoxious birds woke me up. They're so noisy! Did you hear them?"

"Nope, not with my thick walls. You coming to mass with me today?"

"Of course. I'd like to meet Padre Ernesto. Did you know he is Paolo's brother?"

"Humph. I remember."

The two women left the house as the bells tolled in the parish church, beckoning the villagers to Sunday-morning mass. As they approached the church, Maria breathed heavily. Going up the stone steps wasn't easy for her, while Sandra moved effortlessly. Noticing Maria's difficulty, Sandra stopped to give her a chance to rest with the pretext of commenting on the architecture of the building. "What a beautiful church," Sandra observed. "It's holding up well after sitting here over 300 years. The facade reminds me of a woman's face—and those marble baroque flourishes on each side look like long hair flipped up on the ends. Sort of like a Picasso abstract portrait."

"How do you see that? *Che fantasia*!" Maria mused. Sandra lent her arm to Maria and they continued toward the entrance of the church.

Padre Ernesto saw them enter the dark sanctuary that smelled of candle wax, and knew that the young woman with Maria was once the baby he had arranged to be adopted by his brother, Paolo. Now this young woman sat on a pew with her biological mother, her eyes fixed on him, smiling like a long-lost relative. Padre Ernesto felt uneasy seeing them there together. Did she know how he had arranged for her adoption? Had Maria told her daughter of his collaboration to turn her over to his brother and wife? Does she know who her father is? As he realized the mysterious connections, he felt queasy, as if he had just drunk sour milk.

He remembered the boy—Sandra's biological father. Padre Ernesto was the only person that knew the paternity of Sandra besides Maria and her mother, who were unaware of his surname. Not even the boy knew about Maria's pregnancy. The Montesi knew nothing about the boy even though they needled Padre Ernesto endlessly to find out who Sandra's father was.

The interweaving of these lives was like a loosely woven shroud with missing stitches. He recalled the day, nineteen years ago, when the boy came to church to confess. Confession was between the priest and the sinner—shared with no one. This was a sacred oath all priests commit to, and Padre Ernesto took his vocation seriously. He would not share this confession even with his own brother, who was now the legal parent of Sandra.

After the confession, Padre Ernesto never saw the boy again. He didn't remember the boy's name, but he did remember the nervousness in the boy's voice when he told him what he had done to his classmate and how he was surprised how she fought back. He remembered the boy's sincere remorse for succumbing to the bullies. "I feel so stupid. I didn't know what I was doing. I was so mad at them always making fun of me. But, how dumb of me." Padre Ernesto told the boy his sin was forgiven. "You are a boy, and boys have these urges for pretty girls. It's nature's way." But the boy confessed it wasn't for passion. "No, Padre. I did it because the boys kept teasing me and because I wanted them to stop. I didn't want to hurt that girl. I was such a fool."

"God forgives you. You have repented. Now go in peace but don't do it ever again."

"No. I won't, Padre! I do repent! Thank you."

Padre Ernesto was unaware of Maria's pregnancy when the boy came to confess. Then, two months later, Maria's mother came, asking him to help find a solution for her daughter's condition. She didn't tell Padre who had raped her daughter and he respected her wish for privacy. He knew his vows and obligations as a priest, and any secrets and confessions would be his alone to know and protect, at any cost. Sometimes the consequences were tragic, but he kept within him countless confessions and admissions of guilt, no matter how much the truth could help to liberate and atone. The truth was suppressed, and the sinners were content to hear they were pardoned, forgiven, and cleansed of guilt, free to leave the church in the grace of God without consequences. That is how

Checco felt after his confession. He walked out into the light of the Mediterranean sun feeling weightless, smiling, and moving along, onward with his life and plans. He had been forgiven by God, and he didn't know that he had impregnated Maria or how she was suffering.

Padre Ernesto put two and two together. The timing of the boy's confession and the plea for help with an unwanted pregnancy due to rape, in such a small village, was proof enough to know the perpetrator and the victim. Maria was the classmate, and she had been withdrawn from school soon after the boy's confession. It was as clear as the blue sea.

As the memories flooded Padre Ernesto's mind, he avoided Sandra's gaze, and after delivering an unimpressive mass, he quickly disappeared. Sandra wanted to meet Paolo's brother. She thought of him as a relative, and was disappointed to miss the opportunity to introduce herself. Later in the day, after Maria went to oversee the cooking in her trattoria, Sandra returned to the church for confession, to meet Padre Ernesto, and to fortify herself before telling Maria her news. It would be hard to conceal her excitement mixed with apprehension. She wanted to reveal only her pure happiness, untainted by fear. Perhaps the announcement would be easier if she faced Maria with the blessing of Padre Ernesto. She had never gone to confession, but knew the process and was prepared to say the words by rote.

When she sat in the confessional booth, she sensed the presence of Padre Ernesto behind the worn purple curtain. Father Ernesto could see Sandra through a narrow opening in the curtain and braced himself, though he didn't know why he was so apprehensive.

"Forgive me, Father, for I have sinned."

"Do you repent?"

"For whatever mistake I've made, yes, I repent."

"But you must know your sin and repent for that."

"Father, I don't know if I have sinned, but I hope I haven't, and if I have, I want to be absolved."

"You can't be absolved for a sin you are unaware of. You can't repent without a reason."

"It's for Maria—my biological mother. She may be really angry with me. I'm afraid she won't approve, but I'm getting married. It seems it happened so fast, but I've loved him since we met. Now she's the only family I have left, and I don't want to make her upset with me or hurt her. She has already suffered enough in her life. My fiancé is a bit older and has been my tutor, so people could gossip, and Maria hates gossip as much as she resents men. But he's wonderful. If she will get to know him without prejudice, she will know he is good for me."

"I understand your concern, but it is not a sin to be in love. It is not a fault that he happens to be your teacher. The age difference you referred to is not so uncommon here. Only you can know if your decision came from love, and if your love is based on our Christian values, then you needn't be absolved. You have not sinned for being in love."

"Please take my worry as a confession, Padre. I need to feel confident when I see Maria and tell her—it's hard to explain—it happened so fast, and yet we both always knew our relationship was really special. She warned me about making such a hasty decision. I never forgot that—it was so important to her."

"Sacred love has a way of resolving all," Padre Ernesto said. "You are the only one who can decide if the love is right. Maria will accept your decision." He granted the rite of absolution. "Go in peace. Amen, thanks be unto God."

Sandra crossed herself and parroted Padre Ernesto's words, "Amen, thanks be unto God. Thank you. Padre, I know Paolo was your brother, and I wanted to tell you what a good person he was, and his wife too. They told me how you arranged for my adoption, and I understand it was the right decision—so does Maria. Thank you."

Padre Ernesto sat in his dark niche without responding to Sandra's kind message. He felt something was strange, but didn't know what it was. As Sandra walked out of the dark church into the warm sunlight, she felt boosted by her "confession." Without apologies or justifications, she could now tell Maria she was going to marry the right man even if it had been a hasty decision. She thought to herself, "If she is upset, so be it. Nothing can ruin our happiness. It's a gift that I will protect. And Padre Ernesto said she'll trust my decision."

As Sandra walked toward Maria's house, she felt high and light, like the angels painted on the ceiling of the church. "I am so fortunate." She felt her love like music within her—the most beautiful music she had ever heard.

# The Recital

Parents and relatives took their seats in the church's hall that was used for social gatherings in Catania. The wood paneling and beamed ceiling favored the acoustics for the musical event, and the old grand piano was worthy of the young musicians' talent. Sandra was one of eight students, ages nine to thirteen, who would perform. She was the youngest but also the favorite of her teacher, who was about to present the program. As the door of the hall began to close, a stout woman wearing a plain, black dress entered, appearing to be lost as she stopped and scanned the room. Paolo Montesi rose from his folding chair and walked toward the woman, who seemed relieved to see him. He accompanied her to a seat next to him and his wife. She plopped down on the folding chair that shifted and squeaked under her weight, drawing attention to her presence.

The first student, a bored-looking boy, was introduced. "Filippo has chosen to play 'Hall of the Mountain King' by Edvard Grieg." Filippo sat on the piano bench like a little king on his throne. He hammered out the notes with authority, but the loud pounding convinced no one of his skill, except for his parents who clapped with enthusiasm at the end of his piece.

"Thank you, Filippo. Next are the sisters Beatrice and Cecilia. They will play a duet, 'Canon in D' by Pachabel." The girls sat down on the piano bench together as the older of the two looked suspiciously at her sister who smiled back with confidence. They began to play their parts they had practiced so many times together, but the younger sister failed to repeat a refrain, and left the older sister lost, not knowing how to pick up the notes to follow her sister's meandering deviation from the score. She stopped playing in bewilderment as the little sister kept playing, cobbling together random notes, making the older sister seem to be the one that lost her place and given up. The performance ended in embarrassing silence as the big sister slithered off the bench, seething. The little sister stood with dignity and exited smiling, as if all had gone well.

"Things do happen," the teacher announced with humor. Now, Sandra is our next performer. She will play 'Ballata in sol Maggiore' by Frederich Chopin."

Sandra walked toward the piano with graceful gravitas. Her shining black hair was styled in a bun on the crown of her head and her ivory-colored dress made her seem older than her age.

She sat down with purpose on the piano bench, and silently concentrated on the keyboard before raising her hands poised above the keys. Already, the audience felt something special was about to happen. The ensuing notes expressed pensive precision, rife with controlled emotion, perfectly timed. She knew the music intimately and her purpose there was to share it, to reveal all the colors and complexity of Chopin's composition that exalts his patriotism and love of Poland. As the theme developed, her mastery of technique and interpretation moved the audience. Some gasped and stared in amazement as the notes moved from melancholy exploration to a culmination of feverish explosion. Many wondered how such a young girl could know or understand these emotions. What experiences in her young life could she have lived to give her the maturity to express a wide range of musical language so eloquently? A deafening silence settled in after the final chords resonated through the hall. Then the audience burst into applause as Sandra arose and demurely bowed before walking off the stage while the clapping continued.

At the end of the recital, the students joined their parents for the refreshments in the hall. Sandra walked toward her parents wondering who the woman was with them. She didn't look like any of their friends whom she had met at parties in their home.

"Sandra, we have a surprise for you. This is Maria. We didn't want to distract you before the recital by telling you, but we invited her to join us for this special occasion."

Sandra knew who Maria was. Only recently had she consented to meeting her—an idea her parents had proposed.

As Sandra looked at her biological mother, she made an effort to hide her shock. She was nothing like the woman she had imagined. Maria stared back, starstruck by Sandra's beauty and talent. No words were spoken, but the silent thoughts didn't need to be uttered.

"Well, then," Paolo said as he took his iPhone out of his pocket. "Sandra, smile! A memory of your first recital!" He took a picture and put the phone back in his pocket.

"Do you use the internet, Maria?"

"No. Don't have time or computer."

"Then I'll make a print and mail it to you."

"Good idea!" Elena said. "Now let's get some refreshments. I see they have the pastries you loved so much, Maria."

Elena and Paolo Montesi aptly conversed to avoid awkward moments of silence. Sandra and Maria were both filled with questions but words would not emerge even if there was a chance to talk.

"My train . . . I have a train back home soon. Time to go," Maria stammered.

"Thank you for coming," Elena replied. Paolo accompanied Maria to the door, then joined his wife and daughter, relieved the good deed had been fulfilled.

# Prelude

The recital was a turning point for the Montesi family. After Maria left, the piano teacher approached them, teeming with enthusiasm and compliments for Sandra's extraordinary performance. *"La vostra figlia e' bravissima.* The best I've ever had. She has a special talent." Elena already was aware of Sandra's gift as she thanked the music teacher for the kind words. "We're very proud of Sandra. It helps to have a good piano in our home, but I think Sandra would've found a piano somewhere if we didn't have it. The piano fascinated her when she was a baby, and she began touching the keys as soon as she could walk!"

"She must have inherited that from you, Signora Montesi. We all know how well you play."

"Well, I think that is quite impossible—Sandra was adopted, but she has heard me play often. Her biological mom was never interested in hearing me play."

The music teacher smiled in response, not knowing how to react to this candid revelation. Signora Montesi aptly directed the conversation in a different direction. "Thank you for arranging this wonderful event for your students. It has been so delightful to hear all of them. Who knows if Sandra will want to continue with the piano lessons. She, of course, is free to pursue piano playing or not, but if she chooses to do so, we'll support her in every way we can. Girls don't have to worry so much about earning a living!"

Sandra wasn't interested in the refreshments or mingling and nudged Paolo. He understood the cue. "It has been a lovely event, but it's time to get our pianist home."

During the ride home, Sandra didn't wait to say what was on her mind. "Mom—why did you say, 'If I want to pursue piano lessons?' You know I do. And I would've liked to have known ahead of time that I would meet Maria tonight. That was so weird. We didn't have a chance to talk, and she left so early . . ."

"We thought this was the perfect time to invite her," Paolo broke in. "We think she was happy to come for your recital and meet you, but she seemed to be in a hurry to get back to Lento. She probably had other plans there. And of course we know how much you want to pursue piano lessons. Sometimes, we say things just to make conversation. It's a social skill that Elena is very good at."

Paolo's words sounded like an untuned piano to Sandra. She answered with silence.

# Crescendo

As time moved on, the waning harmony of the Montesi family was replaced with dissonance. Elena and Paolo were almost sixty when they adopted Sandra, and now at thirteen, Sandra's independent spirit created attrition with her parents' conservative upbringing. The nine-year-old girl in the ivory dress and prim updo now wore torn jeans and black T-shirts. Her dark, curly hair surrounded her face like storm clouds.

The physical surroundings of the Montesi home that Maria had found so alien were Sandra's natural element. Her inherent need for beauty and intellectual curiosity drew her to the cultural accoutrements of the household. Elena and Paolo purchased artwork and furnishings to create the right social tone that would express their status, but Sandra interacted with the paintings beyond their superficial appearance. Elena played classical music skillfully, but Sandra ventured beyond the pages of music and experimented with chords and melodies that came from within her. She didn't need the scores with their musical signs for "adagio" or "forte" to play the piano. Her sense of timing with her emotions and thoughts naturally resulted in an original piece of music, seemingly without effort.

Elena was perplexed when she listened to Sandra's improvised playing. "What is that you're working on?" she asked.

"I'm not working on anything, Mom."

"Well, I've never heard that piece. Who composed it?"

"No one. I'm just playing what I feel I want to play."

"Sandra! That's really beautiful! You should study composition."

"Maybe someday I will."

"Of course—you'll be a composer someday! A woman composer."

Elena also noticed which paintings Sandra was drawn to. The Sicilian painter Renato Guttuso was getting a lot of attention in the art market. His paintings were commanding high prices, which made them enviable items to own—just the sort of product the Montesis aspired to display in their home. They purchased a landscape scene of the Sicilian countryside that Sandra sometimes lingered in front of, staring at the painting as if listening to it.

"Do you like that one, Sandra? You know it's quite valuable."

"What do you think of it, Mom, besides its value?"

"To me it represents a successful artist with a fashionable political point of view. It's very chic to be communist, you know . . . and Guttuso is a self-proclaimed communist, which is fodder for conversation in our circle. But, he's especially known for his affair with the wife of a wealthy industrialist who is a bonafide capitalist, in Milan! She is so—"

"But, Mom, I mean the value of the painting itself—not for who Guttuso is or what he does. When I look at this painting, I feel the warmth of the dusty path lined with the ficchi d' India cacti. I can almost smell the wild chamomile blooming around the rocky hill. And, that contadino with his mule—they are an integral part of the landscape—the colors seem to move in torrents with and around them as they trod up the path. Each part of the painting is inseparable from the other. I love the unity and the energy and warmth of chromatic expression."

"I didn't see that. What an interesting description, Sandra. Brava."

"I think of Maria when I look at it. She is so quiet but is expressive anyway. I think of her a lot lately. I only met her once. Can we invite her to come here to visit? I want to know more about her."

"Oh, Sandra. We don't want you to be disappointed—it's understandable that you're curious, but she is very closed, and different from us. She hasn't shown interest in you. It was her decision to give you up as soon as you were born, and we think it's better to leave it at that."

Sandra didn't respond, and she didn't leave it at that. Elena's terse words had struck another sour note.

# Fugue

Three more years went by until Sandra informed her parents that she would visit Maria in Lento. She was now sixteen and planned to take the train on her own. Paolo and Elena knew it was useless to try to change her mind and gave Sandra Maria's address.

"Lento is a picturesque village—why don't you take your boyfriend, Luigi, with you? We don't want you going there all alone."

"But I won't be all alone. I'll be with Maria. I don't need Luigi. And, he's not my boyfriend. We just hang out."

Luigi wasn't the only boy in Sandra's school who was attracted to her, but he was the boldest. Sandra didn't admire that quality, but with it he paved his way into her world. He invited himself to the Montesi house to study with Sandra and stayed for dinner sometimes at Elena's invitation. In his mind, Sandra was his girlfriend, and his cocky boasting about the friendship kept the other boys from asking her out. The Montesi liked his self-assured attitude and the fact that he came from a very wealthy family, even though his rough ways sometimes irked Elena.

When he put his glass of soda on the piano, Elena quickly picked it up and informed him that a piano is not a table.

Sandra felt he made himself a little too much at home by the way he strutted into the kitchen and grabbed an apple from the fruit bowl without asking, as if it was his to take—like a barbarian usurping conquered territory. In fact, his blue eyes were the result of the Norman invasion in Sicily that injected the recessive gene into the dark-eyed descendants of Arabs and Greeks. There were other nuances of behavior she didn't like, but she tolerated him because of Elena's encouragement.

Paolo offered to drive Sandra to Lento but he was quickly turned down. He didn't try to argue but stared back at his tall daughter, her wild, bristly hair, her black fingernail polish, and tattered jeans. In his older age, he had given up trying to control her. "Va bene, but let her know before you show up there."

Sandra went to her room to write a letter. "Dear Maria, I am planning to come to Lento to see you November 1, on All Saints holiday. I'm arriving by train that arrives at 11:45 a.m. I'll be alone. I hope this is a good time for you, and that I am not imposing. Looking forward to seeing you! Sandra."

# Andante Con Espressione

Sandra stepped off the train, holding her backpack in one hand, then slung it over her shoulder. Seven years had passed since meeting Maria at the recital. She didn't expect to see her waiting at the station but immediately recognized the short, imposing figure clad in black, planted on the platform. She slowly approached this stranger who had given birth to her.

"Buongiorno, Maria!" Sandra saw a faint gleam in Maria's eyes. This trip had a purpose. Sandra had often anticipated this meeting and thought about what she would say, what she might learn . . . but in this moment, she was not sure if Maria would be willing to talk with her about the past.

"Good morning," Maria blurted. "Andiamo—we'll have some lunch in my trattoria."

"Your trattoria?"

"Si, Sandra. Mia trattoria."

Trattoria Da Maria was once a bread shop that Maria had converted into the eatery. She hired the contractors her father had worked for, who repaired the stone walls and restored the original tiled floor. The gaping bread ovens were replaced with a commercial gas range. Wooden rafters were sanded and stained, and fresh plaster painted white covered the wall that had been too crumbled to salvage. Sandra followed Maria out of the piazza and down the narrow cobblestone street until she saw the quaint sign above the door promising genuine home-cooked food. Upon entering, she admired the cozy interior. Wood shelving was filled with wine bottles interspersed with terra-cotta vases from a local ceramic factory holding Maria's plants she started from cuttings.

"I didn't know you had a business!"

"A lot of things you don't know, Sandra."

They entered the busy locale that was especially busy on the holiday of All Saints. Many diners, dressed in black, had been to the cemetery to honor the saints, and the dead, who lived virtuous lives. Maria led them to a table in the corner set with thick, white plates on butcher-paper placemats. Sandra felt at ease with Maria in the pedestrian atmosphere. A waiter came to pull out their chairs and greeted Maria warmly, with a professional demeanor. They settled into the chairs as the waiter left to get the bread and mineral water for the table.

"Oh, I brought you something!" Sandra took an envelope out of her backpack and handed it to Maria, who pulled the contents out. She looked at the picture in amazement. "It's for me?"

"Yes! Remember when Paolo took the picture at my recital? He sent it with me to give to you. He said he's very sorry he never mailed it like he promised. Better late than never!"

Maria tried to suppress her emotion. Strong feelings scared her. She managed to say "Thank you," and Sandra noticed the pinched smile that Maria couldn't hide.

The waiter placed a basket of bread in front of Sandra. It smelled like the golden grains that grew in the fields nearby. Maria had planned the menu and nodded to the waiter that they were ready to be served. He punctually complied, and returned with two steaming dishes of homemade pasta with local "cima di rape"—the tender, bitter turnip greens. He grated pecorino cheese over the plates, and added, "Buon appetito!" with a smile.

"How long have you had this place?" Sandra asked as she scooped the orecchietti pasta up with her fork.

"Since you were nine . . . when I heard you play the piano. The Montesi . . . good people . . . helped me get started.

"They didn't tell me."

"Why did you come here?" Maria asked bluntly.

Sandra looked directly into Maria's eyes and asked, "Why did you give me away? You are my mother."

They put their forks down and a gravid silence ensued until Maria could respond.

"Life can push you down. It takes over, gives you no choice. You might think you can choose, but life chooses for you. It tricks you to do what it decides, then it blames you later. You trust it at the time."

"Do you mean you regret giving me away?"

"Life gave you away. Then, it was best for you and me and the Montesi. If you happened when I was older, when I could work, had a husband, I would have not thought to lose you. But life threw me down. A horrible boy threw me down. He stole my life and you from me. He stole all my future children from me. I didn't know when you were taken from me, that with you went all hope for the family I thought I'd have someday. And, I don't choose to be angry or to hate, but I hate with all my soul the boy that did that to me. He laughed, and went on with his life—like what he did was nothing. I don't know what happened to him. He doesn't even know he made me pregnant—he has no idea. He has no idea how I hate him."

Maria's words provoked empathy in Sandra, but were chilling at the same time.

"Maria, don't feel bad. I understand. Life doesn't think about what's fair or not. It does what it wants, and then we pay."

Maria was stoic and solid as she took Sandra's hands into hers and squeezed them tightly. Her solemn words came from a deep, dreary place of sorrow. "Sandra. You are young and good. I pray you will find love. That would be enough for me. That would be my happiness. But be careful and wait for the right man, no matter how long you must wait. Never, EVER let yourself be led down the wrong path. Take the time to be sure he is good."

Maria's solemn words weighed on Sandra. She accepted them and carried them like a heavy gift. A powerful force flowed through their grasp as they sat absorbing emotions, holding each other's hands. It was like music—a song with no words, uniting them with a common bond: an atavistic connection that Sandra nor Maria had ever experienced. When they released their hands, the tension relaxed and they enjoyed the meal together like close friends.

Sandra felt emboldened to ask Maria the big question she came with. "Paolo and Elena have never said anything about who my father was—I asked them because I've been wondering about him. They said they don't know anything about him. What happened to him, who is he, where is he?"

"I don't know anything about him now or where he went. I put a stone on him and his name. He knows nothing about you. My mother knew that if we denounced him it would only make things worse. The shame would've been put on us for what happened. The gossipers would've blamed me and my family, as if I caused him to do what he did. We just wanted to hide and avoid the disgrace."

"So he doesn't know about me! Maybe he'd want to know me. Maybe he'd be sorry for what he did. Wouldn't it help if he apologized and showed you his remorse? You must heal and forgive him to be happy and put the bad feelings in the past."

Maria frowned at the thought, and Sandra saw passions in her eyes that she had never seen: hatred and anger. "He used me and threw me away—never apologized. He has no soul, he is evil."

"But Maria, he should have been told. And I have a right to know who my father is, no matter how bad he may be. I'm sorry you have suffered so much, but I need to know who he is. Maybe I'd hate him too, or maybe he would be happy to know he has a daughter. Maybe he'd be sorry for what he did, and he would tell you. We don't know what he's like now, and I want to find out. Tell me his name. Please."

A frightening noise broke the tense conversation. Someone had bumped into the waiter who carried a tray of stacked plates and glasses that crashed on the floor.

As the waiter bent down to pick up the pieces, Maria picked her words to answer Sandra's question. She enunciated each word coldly, keeping them at a safe distance, avoiding the pain they could inflict on her.

"I don't remember his last name. We called him Checco. He left Lento to go to high school in another town. I've heard nothing about him or where he is. That's all I can say."

Sandra saw the searing pain this brought to Maria, and Maria saw the disappointment cloud around Sandra, who was sorry she had brought back Carmela's painful memory.

"It's OK, Maria. I have you . . . you are my mother. That's enough for me. "

Sandra's words were like aloe on a burn. Maria glowed.

After lunch, Maria took Sandra to see a tourist attraction—the natural spring of fresh water—the fonte di Aretusa. The spring of fresh water is enclosed with a high circular wall of stones and sits next to the shoreline of the sea. "There is a legend here in Lento about this spring," Maria began. "Aretusa was a pretty nymph, almost as pretty as you. She was on a hunt with the goddess Diana on a hot day and she wandered off from the hunt and came to the river, Alfeo. Alfeo was so clear, she could see the pebbles at the bottom. She took off her clothes to swim but as soon as she jumped in, the water began to pull her under. She tried to get away, but the river wanted her and turned into a handsome man whose eyes were full of lust. Aretusa called Diana for help, and Diana turned her into this spring to save her. But Alfeo was left alone with his desire for Aretusa. The gods felt sorry for him and turned him back into a river that flowed next to the spring, to be united with Aretusa."

"What a sad story!"

"It's just a legend, but it's also a lesson—don't wander off the path, because it can be dangerous."

"I know, but in the end, Alfeo ended up with Aretusa anyway, and in his original form, but Aretusa didn't become a girl again, she remained a spring! That wasn't fair."

"Well, that's what the gods wanted, and that is how it is—the legend. Now, I think it's about time for your train. I'll walk you to the station."

When Sandra returned to Catania that evening, Paolo and Elena were waiting at the train station. She expected a barrage of questions but found them to be cautiously curious, and unusually reserved.

"How was your day?" Elena asked.

"I'm glad I went!" Her enthusiasm was answered with silence.

"Mom, don't you want to know how Maria is? She's doing great. We had lunch at her trattoria—I loved it! She told me how you helped her start it—you never told me that.

We had a good talk. You were afraid I'd be disappointed, but instead, we got to know each other and she was really nice."

"We're glad to hear she is doing well."

"She told me about what happened, why I was born . . . I can tell she suffers a lot about that, and she has never forgiven that boy."

"Well, it's all water under the bridge now. We all must go on with our lives and be grateful that's in the past."

"But her past was terrible, and she lives with it every day. She's very bitter about that boy. He ruined her life."

"It's just as well that he disappeared, and there's nothing we can do about it. We have no idea who he was and it's best to leave it at that. Maria nor her mother would ever talk about it."

"I put salt in her wounds—I wanted to know about him, but I saw how much it hurt her to talk about it."

"Sometimes it's best not to talk—acqua in bocca!" (water in your mouth) Paolo concluded. He pressed his lips together tightly and jutted out his chin—the typical Sicilian gesture originating with the Camorra, of one who will not talk for fear of retribution.

The Montesi closed the discussion. When they got home, Paolo and Elena went to bed but Sandra went to the piano for solace and sat in silence. The moon shone through the large picture window and illuminated the ivory keys. She thought of the opera "Norma" by Catania's composer, Vincenzo Bellini, and the sheer purity of Casta Diva—the aria sung to the Moon goddess by Norma, who pled for peace and mercy. Sandra needed peace too, and someone to feel close to. Maria had listened to her and responded to her questions, though it hurt to do so. They had an authentic conversation. Maria had talked to her without judgment. It was real.

She put her right hand on the keyboard and played a few notes, repeating them in different variations—until her left hand joined in, striking low chords, complementing the melody. Each note that formed the melody was like a letter of the alphabet, that when put together formed sentences and paragraphs. Finding the right combinations was like speaking honestly, openly, clearly, and sharing a thought with someone there, willing to listen. The sensual synergy with the phrases and sounds she produced gave her a powerful feeling of immense pleasure.

"I will study composition," Sandra decided.

# Legato

"Today would be a good day to stay at home," Elena announced. The air quality index is 85—really bad.

My throat is already irritated from being outside for ten minutes. The pollution is terrible. Not to mention Etna—it's erupting from its southeast crater, and it's a bad one—a paroxysm! There will be lava fountains and flows and ash to add to the existing pollution."

Sandra grabbed her iPhone to Google . . . "paroxysm," she read. "A paroxysm is a sudden and powerful expression of strong feeling, especially one that you cannot control. It can be used to describe expressions of anger, grief, pain, or other emotions. For example, you could say 'He went into paroxysms of laughter' or 'She suffered a paroxysm of coughing.'"

"I think I had a paroxysm last night. I decided to study composition."

"Excellent idea. As a matter of fact, I've already started looking for the best tutor in town."

That same day, Elena called the Istituto Musicale Vincenzo Bellini, where she had studied many years ago, and asked the director for an appointment with the professor of composition.

"Yes, Signora Montesi. That would be Dr. Francesco Verga. His classes should be over by 4:30, and I could arrange for you to meet him today."

"Oh benissimo! It'd be a pleasure."

Elena drove the Fiat to the conservatory and parked in the tiny lot behind the school. There was a strict rule that no one could enter the school while classes were in session because students were practicing, but an exception was made for Elena Montesi. The director met her at the reception. "Please come with me. Have a seat in his office. I'll let Professor Verga know you are here."

As Elena waited, she noticed the tidiness and pleasant atmosphere of Professor Verga's office space. "Just like a composer," she thought to herself. "Everything in its place, neat and harmonious." A healthy fiddle-leaf fig plant with glossy leaves flourished in a planter in the corner of the office, exposed to just the right amount of light. Engravings of monumental buildings of Catania as well as an oil painting of Mount Etna in eruption were in identical frames, hung together on the wall in perfect alignment behind his desk. "

The door opened and Dr. Verga stepped in. She expected a stout, serious fellow with thick glasses and gray hair. Instead, this young professor was tall and athletic looking with wavy black hair and warm dark eyes. He reached out to shake her hand, and sat down behind his desk, situating himself on the chair to listen attentively.

"Allora . . . you are looking for a tutor for your daughter, I hear. She is sixteen?"

"Please don't think I'm presumptuous for asking you, but my daughter is quite talented and has shown a very keen interest in composition. I think she deserves the best teacher we can find, and that's why I've come here to speak with you. Verga . . . is your family related to our famous author born in Catania?"

"No, Signora. I can't claim that honor."

"I would not have been surprised—literature is related to musical composition, in that music is a language too, expressed in notes instead of letters."

"So true!"

"We'd prefer to have a private tutor come to our home. We think Sandra is too young for the university environment. You are very much esteemed—we'd be honored if you would accept this position."

Signora Montesi was convincing and obtained what she wanted. Within the week, Professor Verga rang the bell of the Montesi home to meet his new student.


Dear Maria,

I hope you're well. Lunch at your trattoria was delicious. Elena and Paolo are happy to hear of your success. I not only enjoyed our visit, I cherish it. Let's try to see each other more often from now on. When are you getting internet? We could write without waiting for the postman to deliver the mail—I don't mind writing letters, but using the internet is so much faster! I now have a private tutor to study composition. I just met him for the first lesson. I'm excited to learn how to put the notes in my head down on paper. I hope to hear from you, when you have time. Think about the internet idea!!

Cari Saluti,
Sandra


Sandra took the letter with her to school the next day to post after school before Elena picked her up. She felt resentful that she needed to hide this from her parents, but didn't want to have to defend her need to keep in touch with Maria. Nor did she want to hear their insinuations about Maria that served no purpose other than to berate Maria and discourage Sandra from getting to know her. She slipped the envelope into the postbox and walked back to the school entrance to meet Elena, enjoying the accomplishment of her secret mission. She imagined the letter arriving in Maria's mailbox in Lento and her surprise to find it.

Elena saw Sandra walking toward the car from a different direction that she usually came from out of school. "Where have you been?"

"I got out a little early today and wanted to take a walk."

"The pollution today is at red alert. You should avoid being outside no more than absolutely necessary."

"Well, we can't stop breathing. I already feel suffocated by this place even without pollution. It's terrible to worry about going outside because of bad air. I wonder if Maria is affected down in Lento?"

"Let's just worry about Catania, where Etna is a stone's throw. How did your first lesson go with Professor Verga? He seems nice."

"I like him. I think he'll be great. Are you sure the bad air is just from Etna, or is Etna a scapegoat for pollution caused by the petrol industry here? And have you seen the water along the coast—full of industrial waste near the port? It's so sad. But, don't you think all the traffic and diesel engines may have something to do with the bad air?"

"Our new mayor has promised to fight pollution— we'll see . . . We're having a few friends over for aperitifs this evening. Why don't you get yourself cleaned up and join us."

"Oh no, I wanted to start studying the lessons Professor Verga left for me . . . I read the new mayor has also promised to fight for business. Which will be more important to him? Let me guess . . . I'm afraid his two objectives contradict each other."

"Sandra! Don't make assumptions. Luigi's parents are coming this evening and I heard he'll probably come as well. Come down, at least to see Luigi. Don't disappoint him, or me."

"I really don't care if he's disappointed or not, and I wish you wouldn't encourage him to come here. He acts like I'm his girlfriend, and I don't even like him. And why are you still having these parties when this virus is so dangerous? You refuse to get the vaccine, and while everyone is wearing masks—you don't even do that. "

"This is just another flu. How can we wear masks while we eat and drink, or have conversations with friends? You'll see. In a few weeks, this will be all over and you will have taken those vaccines for nothing."

In a few weeks, a total lockdown took effect, and most everyone followed the orders, except for the Montesi and their circle, who refused precautions. In due course, Paolo and Elena fell ill. They had fevers, wheezed, and coughed up blood, but would not call a doctor.

"I'm going to call an ambulance," Sandra announced.

"Nooooo," Elena wailed. "We need to rest and we'll be fine!" she sputtered. The paramedics came and wheeled them to the ambulance. Paolo was resigned, but Elena's ire was subdued only by her lack of strength. She tried to speak, interrupted by coughing, but managed to stare at Sandra with anger as the gurney was slid into the ambulance. That was the last time Sandra saw them. They were taken to the Cannizzaro Hospital where Sandra's life began, and theirs ended. At nineteen, she was alone in the Montesi house. The only important people left in her life were Maria and Professor Verga.

The end of the lockdown meant new freedom for Sandra, both physical and psychological. She looked forward to seeing her tutor, who was about to arrive for the first lesson after the end of isolation.

# Atonal

When the bell rang, Sandra ran to the door expecting to see Francesco Verga, though it was early for her lesson. She thought it unlike him to come early, he was always precisely on time, but when she opened the door, she was surprised to see Luigi standing there with his squinting blue eyes, assuming she'd be thrilled to see him.

"Why are you here? I have to study, and not with you." Luigi stepped inside without an invitation.

"I thought I'd drop by. It's been a long time, and now you're here all alone without your parents. I heard they died. You must have missed me." He sauntered into the living room and sat on the sofa as if he were the owner of the house. He saw Sandra looking at him with resentment.

"Enne ca" (come here) he ordered, slapping the cushion of the sofa. Sicilian dialect lacks the vowels that soften the Italian language. He chose to speak in dialect instead of saying "Vieni qua" in Italian that has a lilting sound instead of his harsh "Enne ca" that sounded so sharp it could cut stone.

Sandra sat down to confront him, to tell him to stop coming to her home, but as she began to speak, he understood her intention and shoved her down on the sofa. Even her rush of adrenaline to fight back could not overpower his force. She managed to scream "Aiuto!" before he pressed his hand over her mouth. She kicked her leg out, and the glass coffee table crashed in a thousand pieces on the terrazzo floor.

She didn't hear the front door pushed open. Suddenly, Luigi was pulled off of her and someone punched him in the face. Luigi ran off like a dog with its tail between its legs as Professor Verga reached down to pull her up. She embraced him as he wrapped his arms around her. She felt he could protect her from any danger. She had never been so thankful, or felt so safe. The embrace was spontaneous and powerful, like the connection she felt with Maria, grasping her hands when they spoke at the trattoria three years ago.

# Virtuosity

Now that the pandemic was over, Catania opened up to its population, desperate to meet at cafes, dine out, go to parties, and travel. The liberation was exhilarating. Sandra didn't wish to go out into the city, but preferred to go down to swim at the Lido Bamboo, the closest beach to her house. Swimming in the transparent water was exhilarating enough for her. The immaculate beach was equipped with folding chairs and umbrellas—the same beach Maria had gazed down at from her balcony at the Montesi house, seeing only filth associated with her memory of being raped on a stony beach. Not far south was the Cannizzaro Hospital, where Sandra was born. Elena had described to Sandra that frantic evening when she saw her come into the world and called her by name. "Sandra—my daughter." Now Sandra wondered how Maria felt in that moment, and realized her connection with Maria was so different from her relationship with Elena, who had been the ever-domineering presence in her life.

After the incident with Luigi, Professor Verga had become her confidant with whom she could talk freely about her dead adoptive parents and her natural mother. He listened to her speak of her mother's rape, as well as her conflicts with the Montesi. Sandra saw how these revelations emotionally impacted him, especially his empathy regarding her mother's rape. His sensitivity to her narratives brought them closer together.

"And your father? The boy who raped your mother . . . do you know him?"

"No. Maria doesn't want to talk about him. He doesn't know she got pregnant."

"Do you ever wish you could meet him?"

"I do. I so much want to know who he is, no matter who he is, I just need to know. I've always felt something missing in my life. Even if it's something bad I'm missing, it's better to know."

"I hope you will be able to find out and meet him someday. It could give you closure—no matter what he's like."

"Maria doesn't even remember his last name and has no idea where he went, so it's unlikely I'll ever know him."

Professor Verga felt a natural sense of responsibility to protect her. She sensed this as well as his strength and kindness. When he came to Sandra's home for lessons, she met him at the door and always greeted him with "Buongiorno, Professore Verga" until one day he answered, "Call me Francesco."

At the end of the lesson, Sandra invited him to see her plants on the patio that she coddled every day.

"I don't know what I'd do without these friends to take care of! I feel so lonesome sometimes."

"Sandra, come with me to the Conservatory. I want to show you the school. Maybe it's time for you to get back out into the city. Let's go! I'll take you there now."

"Now? I'm not dressed to go out!"

"You look fantastica! Black is classic—can't go wrong."

Sandra was dressed in black jeans and a black sweater, and she used fire-engine red lipstick. Her curly black hair was worked into a single braid that fell in the center of her back.

"You look like the *Gatto Volcanico*—the volcanic cat that holds within it the fire, and the earth of Etna, smoldering, creeping through the streets of Catania."

"That sounds like I'm a potential danger, dormant now, but eruptive later."

"Not at all! You are far from dormant, and the only thing that will explode is your talent and gift to compose!"

Professor Verga opened the door of his Mini Cooper for Sandra to ease into, finding enough space for her long legs. They drove down the hill to Via Etnea, and turned into the little parking lot behind the Conservatory Vincenzo Bellini. The gate opened automatically for his car and he parked in his reserved space. As they walked toward the entrance, Sandra saw the garden next to the Conservatory.

"I didn't know there was a garden here. These trees are incredible! Look at that palm tree. What a huge base for such a slender trunk. Can we go into the garden?"

"Sure, we can go in. Look at those trees with the exposed roots that look like dragon spines."

"Their whole root system seems to crawl and interweave on the surface. Are they banyan trees?"

"Yes—banyans. An Italian botanist brought a plant from a nursery in France—or maybe from Venice, that seems more likely. Mariners brought specimens they collected on their sea journeys to exotic places . . . That plant is growing in Palermo now for over two hundred years. These are its offshoots, probably introduced through the botanical garden just down the road from here."

"Those roots do look like spines of dragons, or the backs of serpentine mythological creatures sleeping on the ground."

"Be careful not to trip on them . . . you could wake them up!" Sandra's eyes narrowed as she smiled at his joke. Francesco Verga had always considered her to be an attractive young woman, but now she was personal and real—like a living concept within him—a human ideal. She embodied his sense of order and beauty.

"I love you, Sandra." The words sounded pure, without expectation or pretense: plain words of truth that had to be spoken.

Sandra felt these words energize her like the warmth of the sun. Her response came from within, like the notes she played that evening, three years ago, thinking of Bellini's "Casta Diva" when Norma invoked the support of the Moon goddess. It was that night that she decided to study composition—the decision that brought Francesco Verga into her life. Like Norma, Sandra also felt a need for love, and now her plea had been answered. "I love you too, Francesco." Her words came easily, as if voicing a fact she had always known.

# Adagio

The transition from a tutor-student relationship to a couple changed little in their physical interaction, which didn't progress beyond an embrace. Their union was strong, based on years of getting to know each other with no doubt about a future together, but sex wasn't a part of their connection. Before Sandra, Francesco had never pursued a relationship with a woman beyond a dinner or movie, and Sandra had never had a date. They spoke of other young couples who rushed into marriage and invested their family's savings in lavish weddings only to divorce after one or two years when passions cooled and they realized marriage wasn't a perpetual dream.

"Francesco, tell me—you must have had a girlfriend before me. You're handsome and caring. There was never someone special?"

Francesco appeared worried before he answered. "It's true, women have flirted with me but the more they insisted, the more space I needed. I've never felt at ease with a woman as I do with you."

They met almost every day when Francesco came out of the conservatory after teaching and walked the city like tourists, sometimes stopping next to the monument to Vincenzo Bellini to read the musical notes etched into the stone base. They played a game of translating the notes into alphabetic letters to form words. "Fa =F, Mi=E, Re= D, Mi=E—that spells FEDE (faith), like the faith I have in you," Sandra mused. "Maybe Bellini was sending cryptic messages or making riddles for us to decipher."

"I don't know if Bellini was religious, but faith without knowledge can be dangerous," Francesco added.

"I wasn't thinking of religious faith—but I agree. Blind faith can be dangerous. I know you well enough to have blind faith in you, but I want to know everything about you—tell me about your parents."

"They live in America. I think you'd like them—they love nature, like you, and they're outspoken, like you. They were unhappy about how things go here in Sicily. I'll tell you all about them some other time."

One hot day when the massive door to the St. Agatha cathedral was open, they walked in to cool off. Francesco pointed out a marble slab engraved with a dedication by Pio X. He squinted to see the words in the dimly lit cathedral and read aloud, "Our greetings to Sicily, ancient civilization resonant with memorable historic events, rich not only of nature's gifts, but also mother of inspiration of superior sagacity. Its population good and exuberant, like the excellent climate of this enchanted island. It has been for centuries strong as its rocks, arduous in its defense of freedom like the fire of its volcanos." He stepped back and addressed Sandra. "This is why I love Sicily. It inspires me. You embody these words. You inspire me."

"Sicily is enchanted and has resisted invasion after invasion, but we have not been able to free ourselves from internal enemies, so we are only half free. And that is why your parents live in the United States. And that is why Maria pays her 'vigilante' every month so her trattoria won't be vandalized."

"You're right, as the dedication says, you are of superior sagacity."

They left holding hands and walked a short distance to sit at a table at Prestipino, just steps away from the Cathedral.

"This seems like a dream, but it's real, Sandra. Every moment we're together is natural and true."

"I feel that way too, Francesco. I know nothing can divide us. I know it's real. I want to tell my mother about us." Sandra stirred sugar into a bold espresso. "I need to go tell her in person, and I hope she'll be happy for me."

"Do you think she may not be?"

"She warned me about making a hasty decision, and letting a boy take advantage of me. I want to tell her how well I know you, but she has such an aversion to men—she's so bitter, suspicious, and angry—she may be unhappy about this and I don't want to upset her. I don't want any darkness over our future."

"Then you should go. Where does your mother live?"

"Lento."

"My parents are from Lento! Let's drive there together."

"That's amazing! Then you know what a lovely place it is . . . We will go together soon, but this time I need to go alone. I want to talk with her first. I'll take the train . . . and some cannoli from here. Elena told me how many she used to eat while she was expecting me!"

"No wonder you're so sweet."

# A Church Without a Roof

When Sandra returned from Lento, Francesco met her at the station. Her smile told him the trip had gone well.

"She's happy for us! Before I told her, I went first to confession, and then we met at Maria's house, where I finally got up the courage to tell her. At first, she didn't say anything and the look in her eyes scared me, but when I told her how we met and how I love you, she relaxed and said she trusted me to know when I met the right man, and now she knows it's you. She's already imagining grandkids! I wish you could've seen how excited she was. She seemed transformed."

"I can't wait to meet your mother. Looks like we'd better start planning our wedding!"

"She has already started the planning . . . We'll be having the reception and lunch in her trattoria! And, I already know where I want our wedding to be. I think you'll agree—you must already know about the church in Lento . . . San Giovanni Battista, in the Jewish quarter.

"Yes—the one without a roof!"

"I like it—open to the sky, with the light of the sun on us while we take our vows instead of closed up in a dark sanctuary . . . just so it doesn't rain."

"Even if it rains, you know the adage, *sposa bagnata, sposa fortunata.*" (A drenched bride brings good luck.)

"And you must know the legend in Lento, of Aretusa . . . she was not such a lucky dripping wet bride!"

"But she wasn't a bride—there was no wedding."

"Such a stickler for details, you are. You're right— no wedding, but they ended up together anyway, just in different forms."

Francesco took Sandra's hand and caressed it. "I'll always love you, no matter what form you may take."

"I would prefer to stay in my human form if possible! Seriously, tell me about your parents. I only know they live in America."

"Have you ever heard of Bloomington, Indiana?"

"I know it's famous for its School of Music . . . Jacob's school."

"Yes. They ended up there in a roundabout way. My father was hired by a pharmaceutical company in Indianapolis, and they moved there while I started graduate school here. Unlike you, my parents were in their thirties when I was born. When my dad retired, they moved down to Brown County, Indiana—it's near Bloomington and the most beautiful part of the state with its rolling hills and forests and lakes. Dad was tired of the problems here—you know that line in the movie *Gianni Stecchino* . . . when a taxi driver says—'there's a problem here in Palermo . . . a very big problem . . . traffic!' Of course he didn't mean traffic. The Camorra affects almost everyone who has a business, no matter how small. He wanted to cut ties with that and hoped I'd move to Indiana and maybe teach at Indiana University, but I love Sicily too much to leave. It has soul and history, and it inspires me. I'd feel lost in the woods in Indiana."

"I love Sicily too, but I understand how they feel. Sicily is inspiring, but it's also a bitter place where people are taken advantage of and feel helpless to change it. I can understand your parents' sense of liberation to get away from this oppression. I hope to travel someday and see new places. They will come for our wedding, I hope."

"Of course! I've already told them our news, and they want to know the date. They'll come for sure. They will love you!"

"And my mother will love you! I told her we would come see her next weekend. She said she'll close the trattoria Sunday and we'll meet there for lunch. She's inviting the priest I want to marry us—he's Paolo's brother. I can't think of anyone else I'd want to invite to our wedding, besides your family."

"I agree—it's a family affair."

# Crescendo

B y the time Sunday came, the weather had changed.
Even though Maria had said she wanted to lose
weight, Sandra bought a dozen cannoli while
Francesco waited in the car in Piazza Borsellino, not
far from Prestipino that's in the piazza for pedestrians
only. The pasticceria was crowded on Sunday morning,
as customers who usually sat at the tables outside in the
piazza crowded inside to avoid the rain. The long line
was daunting but finally she rushed back to the car with
the package covered with cellophane. The drive seemed
longer than the train trip. Francesco drove with caution
in the rain along the curving road, but Sandra became car
sick before they arrived.

Parking was a problem in Lento as well, but the rain
had eased to a prickly drizzle. They welcomed the walk to
Trattoria Da Maria. It would give them time to unwind
from the road trip and freshen up for Francesco's first
meeting with Maria. He tried to appear relaxed but Sandra
could see he was nervous. "Compose yourself!" she joked.

"Very funny, Sandra. Good one."

"Don't worry. Maria is totally on board with this. She will welcome you warmly . . . as warmly as she can—just know she may seem reserved and blunt, but she has a big heart."

"It's been so long since I've walked these streets, but not too much has changed, besides new shops and restaurants."

"There's the trattoria—see—down the street, on the left side?"

In that moment a hefty gull dive-bombed them as it swooped down to grab a half-finished brioche left on a table of a café they were passing. Not only was it unnerving, but it left a white slimy goo on Francesco's jacket.

He groaned with exasperation. "This will make a great impression!"

Sandra grabbed a napkin from the table and began cleaning it off with some mineral water at the café. "Don't worry. A little gull poop won't ruin anything. You know it brings good luck!"

Francesco watched her artfully dab at the stain. "If only all these adages were true."

"C'mon. We're almost there." She patted the moist spot. "See? You can hardly tell where it was."

They held hands as they approached the trattoria. When they arrived, Francesco opened the door for Sandra and followed her in. Padre Ernesto looked up from the table he was sitting at in the corner. He appeared disheveled to Sandra. "Buongiorno, Padre—it's a pleasure to see you." Before he could stand up, Maria emerged from the kitchen wearing a new floral-print dress and an auspicious smile. Sandra stepped forward to embrace her and kiss her cheeks. "Ciao, Mamma. You look so pretty in that dress!" Maria appeared uncharacteristically meek and vulnerable.

As Sandra turned to introduce her fiancé, Maria stepped back, staring at Francesco. Her smile slackened as her eyes widened. Francesco stiffened and Padre Ernesto dropped back down on his chair.

Sandra noticed a dizzying shift in the room as if the world had suddenly been jolted off orbit. An uncanny sound coming from Maria astounded everyone.

"CHECCO!" Maria howled. "CHECCO!"

Padre Ernesto covered his face with his hands.

Sandra looked at Francesco, who had become pallid. "What's happening, Francesco?"

"She's the girl I violated when we were thirteen," he gasped. He rushed toward Maria and fell on his knees before her. "I didn't know what I was doing—I was a stupid boy! Maria. Please forgive me! I didn't know you were Sandra's mother.

"*Vai via!*" (get out) Maria shrieked.

"I confessed . . . Padre said I was absolved—but I didn't think of you or how you felt—I should have apologized long ago. I'm so sorry!"

He turned to Sandra, who had transformed from a serene woman into a frightened girl—stunned and silent.

"Sandra, I didn't tell you what I had done because I was too ashamed. I tried to forget that day. When you told me about Maria, it reminded me of what I had done, but I had no idea it was with your mother! As your husband, I'll live the rest of my life to atone for that day."

Maria stood like a statue above him. Her voice thundered. "Checco—you are Sandra's father. I have never been with another man after that."

Francesco arose from his imploring position at Maria's feet and staggered to the table where Padre Ernesto sat with his face still hidden in his hands. He sat down in front of him.

"Padre, did you know?"

Padre Ernesto lifted his face and looked at Francesco. "I did. I could not have imagined you would ever meet Sandra. It's not my job to inform others of my suppositions. Who would ever confess if their words were not protected by sacred privacy?"

Sandra and Maria were now cloistered together at another table across the room. Padre Ernesto arose and went to sit with them as Francesco remained, holding his face in his hands.

He sat next to Maria, and in his priestly persona said, "Maria. What has just happened is a sign from God. It is time for you to forgive, and heal."

"How can I? He ruined my life—stole my future, and now he would steal my daughter and ruin her life too."

Padre Ernesto's bleary eyes focused on Maria. "He didn't know what he did. He made a bad mistake, and he came to confess. He repented soon after what happened. That was long ago. Now he has asked you for your forgiveness."

Sandra took Maria's hand. "Mamma, he protected me from Luigi who almost raped me. He has always been kind and good. I have taken time to know him and love him for who he is. It's different now, of course, but my love is still there. Forgiving him could take a big weight off you—you've carried it for so long." Maria remained silent, clutching Sandra's hand. Sandra looked across the room at Francesco sitting alone, deep in despair.

That is my father, she thought, feeling the shock and pain of losing her fiancé. But she also experienced a wondrous sensation of joy, discovering this extraordinary man is her father. She sat between her parents with bitterness on one side, and agony on the other. Padre Ernesto's words, "a sign from God" rang in her mind like the tolling of a bell. She didn't believe in God out of blind faith, but she did feel a presence of something bigger in the room, something so strong it transcended shame, hatred, and revenge. This uplifting force made her stand up and led her to the middle of the room. She looked from one side to the other.

"I felt something missing in my life. Now I have you, Maria, but I wanted to know my father too. Now I do, and if you had known who he really is, you wouldn't have been angry or filled with hatred all this time. Mamma, come here." Maria stood and moved toward Sandra, who then looked toward the other side of the room. "Francesco . . ." She held her hand to him. He arose and walked to the center of the room. Sandra reached out and took Maria's hand in hers and with her left hand, took Francesco's. Her fervent words erupted in a demanding tone. "Stop your guilt and bitterness. It's time to end those feelings!" A moment of ominous silence followed until Francesco reached out for Maria's hand. She accepted the hand with reserve, holding it like a foreign object, and the three stood in a circle. Maria was unable to retain the tears that made shining paths down her cheeks. She hadn't cried for many years and the release brought a liberating, sweet pain.

Francesco spoke next, gazing at Sandra. "I know how important it was for you to know your father. I'm stunned and honored to be your Dad. When my parents find out, they will be shocked, like we all are, but they'll also be overwhelmed with joy to welcome you to the family. They never thought they'd have a grandchild." Then he looked at Maria. "I will honor you the rest of my life."

Then Maria wiped the tears off her cheeks as she spoke. "I feel a heavy weight come off my heart. My beautiful daughter has a good father and that boy I hated is gone. Today we were going to celebrate an engagement. Now we'll celebrate something else. A lunch was made . . . let's not let good food go to waste!"

Maria's resilience cleared the air and the world seemed to spin back into orbit. Padre Ernesto stood up and began to clap his hands. Francesco and Sandra applauded as Maria began to sob openly, her copious tears draining a reservoir of hatred, flushing out stagnant anger. Like a miracle, she welcomed Francesco's consoling arms around her and she felt her life begin.

The very unusual lunch at Trattoria Da Maria came to a quiet end. The original plan after lunch was for the newly engaged couple to go with Maria and Padre Ernesto to San Giovanni Battista, "The Open Church," to visit the venue and plan the wedding ceremony. There was an appointment with the superintendent to discuss a date and procedure for a small, private wedding that now would not take place.

~~~~~~~~~~~~~~~~~~~~~~~~~~~~~~~~~~~~~~~~~~~

Padre Ernesto walked to the church to cancel the appointment and explain the change of plans. He used the occasion to stand in the open sanctuary and contemplate the extraordinary events of the day. There were no pews in this church with the sky for a ceiling, so he stood facing the altar. His usual place was behind the altar to address a congregation, but this switch of position offered a new perspective.

"Isn't this appropriate," he thought to himself. "Everything is backward today. An engaged man transformed into the father of his future bride instead of becoming her husband. His future bride became his daughter. And Maria has transformed too." He felt humbled standing alone before the altar without his flock around him, with nothing but an open blue sky above, with no preplanned sermon to deliver. He was liberated from his official position and freed from a hidden, gnawing mystery. Something heavy and dark has plagued him since he saw Maria and Sandra together for the first time when they entered his church, and now he felt liberated as if all had shifted into its proper space. Atonement, forgiveness, and love wiped clean the slate of doubt. "Salvation," he whispered. "The truth out in the open has liberated us— the truth, together with love has blessed us."
~~~~~~~~~~~~~~~~~~~~~~~~~~~~~~~~~~~~~~~~~~~

~~~~~~~~~~~~~~~~~~~~~~~~~~~~~~~~~~~~~~~~~~~~~

Francesco lingered in Lento before driving back to Catania, alone. He walked to the house where he had lived with his parents before moving to Catania. "How will I tell them about Sandra, and Maria?" He never told his parents about the taunting of the boys in his class, or his painful vulnerability to them, nor his fateful reaction. He realized he had lived with shame buried within him from the day he took Maria to Cala Rossa. Even though he had been officially forgiven at confession, the forgiveness of Maria was what truly liberated him.

He walked to the beach and down the steps where he had pulled Maria along behind him. Instead of following the wall leading away from the beach, he walked straight to the shore. He picked up stones and began throwing them into the water, one after another. The sounds of the plunging rocks alleviated the weight and pain of the terrible memory.

~~~~~~~~~~~~~~~~~~~~~~~~~~~~~~~~~~~~~~~~~~~~~

Sandra walked to the Fonte of Aretusa, recalling the legend that Maria had recounted when she was sixteen. When she told Francesco about the legend and how Maria had used the story of Aretusa's transformation as a warning, he told her he'd always love her in any form. Now they had all taken new roles with love as the common denominator. She leaned against the stone wall containing the pool and gazed down into the deep limpid water imagining the network of waterways underground providing water for Lento, like veins under the skin, carrying blood in a body. A network carrying such vital liquids, hidden, yet real and essential, inspired a melodic theme for a new composition. As she walked toward the train station, her pace matched the timing of the song while chords and phrases formed in her mind.

When she was home after the most incredible day of her life, she welcomed the solitude and silence that accompanied her in the big house and began putting the notes of "Aretusa's Spring" on paper. Delving into composing and following her musical muse helped her to cope with the shock, and the oddity of finding her father. Tomorrow would be a new day. She would play the freshly penned composition for her tutor and share the significance and repercussions of the astounding revelations with her father. The taut ambiguity of the new relationship twisted her emotions like a Gordian knot.

~~~~~~~~~~~~~~~~~~~~~~~~~~~~~~~~~~~~~~~~~~

After lunch, Maria was left alone. She closed the trattoria and locked the door—the locale would never be the same to her. It too had transformed, into a stage where unimaginable scenes had been enacted, that changed the trajectory of her existence. As she walked home, the narrow street seemed wider and brighter. Later in the evening, she went into the courtyard to tend to her plants. A couple strolled by and watched her watering the plants as they passed. "Buonasera, signori," Maria sang out. The sound of her own voice greeting strangers aroused optimism and joy within her.
~~~~~~~~~~~~~~~~~~~~~~~~~~~~~~~~~~~~~~~~~~

As she prepared for bed, she washed her face and stood in front of the mirror in the bathroom. Breaking with her normal routine, she gazed at her face and studied her features, considering how she must appear to others. The relief she had felt that day made her smile, and she saw herself as an attractive young woman with her life ahead of her. She climbed the narrow steps to the upper bedroom and slept in the bed where Sandra had slept. She left the shutters open. Tomorrow she will wear her floral dress to work and throw away the black one.

# Coda

That solitary, familiar-looking young woman can
only be our granddaughter!" No introductions
were necessary. Mr. and Mrs. Verga recognized
Sandra immediately—not just from the picture
Francesco had texted, but from the way she walked
when she entered the Arrivals area at the Indianapolis
International Airport. Francesco carried himself in the
same style, stepping in harmony with the body, moving
fluidly through space. Sandra also had her father's dark,
expressive eyes that searched the throng of people waiting
for arriving passengers.

All the attendees of the phenomenal lunch at Trattoria
Da Maria had agreed that time and distance was needed
to adapt to their individual transformations . . . to find
footing and balance in their unexpected new lives, so
far flung from original plans and habits. The move to
Indiana was a necessary change of course for Sandra,
who needed to detach herself from the memory of a
fiancé and embrace the reality of paternal love. Living
with her newly discovered grandparents provided that
distant space—yet kept them connected with a bond

of familial blood. Well aware of Sandra's talent, the Vergas purchased an excellent used Steinway piano that was delivered to their getaway cabin on a lake near Bloomington, where Sandra lived in her idyllic dream, surrounded by nature.

She soon became acquainted with other musicians in the area, at the Jacob School of Music and The University of Indianapolis, where she heard about the American Pianists Awards, with its headquarters in Indianapolis. After being encouraged to enter the competition, she was accepted as one of the five finalists and embarked on the gamut of recitals in various venues over the following year to determine the winner.

The experience of competing with the other talented contestants opened up a new world for her. She formed genuine friendships with the pianists who all had ambition to win the prestigious prize, but without attrition or envy. They performed in atriums of hospitals, on the stages of high schools, in foyers of museums, in nursing homes, providing free access to music, enriching the community and inspiring other young musicians. At the end of the year, the finals would take place in the Historic Hilbert Theater on the Circle—the center of Indianapolis, the center of Indiana, known as the "crossroads of America."

As Sandra stood offstage during her introduction for the last performance of the competition, she closed her eyes and took in a deep breath. Behind closed eyes, she saw the clear Ionian Sea, the sunny streets of Catania, the fresh-fruit vendors squeezing orange juice into paper cups for passersby, Paolo and Elena at her first recital, Maria in her black dress, the raucous sea gulls, the exposed roots of the banyan trees, Francesco, and the ominous Mount Etna. The mosaic of images swelled in her as she walked onstage toward the piano. She bowed to the audience before announcing with a slight Italian accent, "I will play something I composed. It's about spiritual and physical transformations, titled 'Aretusa's Spring.'"

The Prelude sounded light, like an exploration into unknown territory, searching to identify a hope and a desire. The optimistic tone then shifted to Crescendo, a growing sense of inquietude and disdain told with vibrantly toned, definitive major chords, in a faster tempo. The intense pace led to another space, Fugue, where the anxiety was released to run free into a new place of Consonance, serene realization. The temporary phase of consonance was broken by the striking contrast – Atonal, terrifying, staccato notes—as sharp as Sicilian dialect and as hard as Sicily's rocky terrain. The frenzy resolved into a warm stream of colorful emotions, tinged with the sadness of minor chords, Adagio, flowing cautiously and slowly to ascertain a new reality. The expected conclusion was cut off, overpowered by a new wave of bold notes, like an epiphany, Crescendo, overruling a complacent perceived finale, changing the narrative of superficial harmony into complex tones sounding of hard truth, Coda, ending in brave confrontation.

The final notes were still resonating through the theater when a wheezing sob, like a snort came from the VIP section in the audience. As Sandra walked offstage, she glanced down to the source of the sob and saw a mortified Maria clutching a handkerchief over her mouth. She was sitting next to the Vergas, and there was Francesco! Who was that young man sitting next to him?

The MC walked across the stage and announced that the jury had reached a decision. The five contestants returned together and stood in a row. Sandra's repertoire throughout the year leading up to this night had included her original compositions, which impressed the judges beyond their esteem for her virtuoso ability. The contestants were all impressive in their unique ways, so, as always, the choice was difficult. The audience waited in suspense while the MC slowly opened the envelope.

This year's recipient of the American Pianists Award is . . . Sandra Montesi.

A reception followed. Mr. and Mrs. Verga guided their guests into the ornate hall with stately windows overlooking the Circle. They had come as a surprise to Sandra. She was amazed to see Maria walking toward her, who looked like a different person after almost two years. She wore an elegant dress that accentuated her lovely figure. Her black curls framed the sculpted lines of her classic Grecian features and glowing eyes. "Mamma!" Sandra exclaimed as she rushed to hug her mother. "You are so beautiful!"

"Oh, Sandra. I feast on happiness now. No need for so many cannoli!"

The Vergas congratulated Sandra gushingly, then turned to Maria. "Please stay as long as you want—you're our daughter-in-law, you know."

Francesco hugged and congratulated Sandra, who could now regard him from a daughter's perspective. He looked different, with an easygoing flair. His gravitas lifted and his spirit shone like sun through an opening in the clouds. He introduced the young man next to him. "This is my partner, Daniele." Sandra embraced him. "It's a pleasure to meet you, Daniele."

Francesco smiled as he watched his daughter welcome his partner. "A lot has happened since you left, Sandra. You must be as surprised as I was. I did some soul searching and realized I never could have been the husband you expected. When I met Daniele, I came to terms with the fact that I am gay. We'll stay in Indianapolis for a few weeks, and Maria will be here too, so we can all get together and celebrate before returning to Catania."

Maria announced she would stay in Bloomington awhile too. "For a well-deserved vacation," added the Vergas. "And, Sandra, soon you will be traveling to perform in venues all over the world. You know this award isn't just monetary—it will support and help launch your career."

"I'm sorry Paolo and Elena weren't here to see this," Sandra said.

Maria thought back to when she was alone, afraid, and angry twenty-one years ago, and how much had changed since the Montesi took her in. "They helped get you here . . . Us here. Thank you, Elena and Paolo."

The Italian family left the theater and lingered in the Monument Circle in the heartland of America, hugging and saying their buona notte. Some people leaving the theater observed the affectionate, animated interaction and summed them up in a few words. "What a typical Italian family!"

Without spoken words, the grandparents, parents, and Sandra understood each other profoundly, knowing they would always be united. They shared a universal language—something beautiful like music that transcends life's fickle tricks of fate—that transcends subversion and hate— like a song that's more powerful than the kindred blood in their veins. They shared a song of love that resonates in everyone, family or stranger, whose heart is open to hear it.